WINTER COWBOY

WHISPER RIDGE, WYOMING - BOOK 1

RJ SCOTT

Love Lane Books

DEDICATION

To Meredith for the cover art that inspired a whole new series set in Whisper Ridge, Wyoming. What did you do!

To Rachel and Vicki for cheering me along. For Elin who picked me up and brushed me down. For Sue who polished me up and made me shine, and to my army of proofers who work so hard.

Love you all. Thank you.

And always for my family.

Winter Cowboy - Whisper Ridge Wyoming #1

Cover design by Meredith Russell. Edited by Sue Laybourn.

Published by Love Lane Books Limited

Winter Cowboy

RJ SCOTT

Love Lane Books

1

DANIEL

2009

A FIGURE STOOD beside Isaac's grave and I knew immediately who it was.

There was no marker yet for the boy who had died two weeks ago and who would be forever nineteen. Flowers marked his resting place, but snow had long since covered them and softened the raised earth so it wasn't as obvious against the gravestones around the figure. A car accident had taken Isaac, killed him on impact, and his family grieved for a future that would never be realized.

I'd just left my brother, Chris, in the hospital, broken beyond repair in the same accident. At least we had the possibility of a future with him, even though the road to recovery would be hard. He was still in a medically induced coma, not yet awake to know he'd lost his leg, or that fire had marked his face. But he would wake up. They told us he'd live.

No one had asked me where I was going when I'd left Chris' room, each of us lost in various stages of shock and grief, and we all dealt with what had happened in our own way. I'd needed to connect with Isaac. Needed the peace to balance the loss and guilt that ate away inside me.

Isaac dead on impact, Chris' future destroyed, and in front of me, hunched over Isaac's last resting place, was the man responsible for it all.

The man who left my bed in the dead of night to become a murderer.

Micah.

He was huddled into his coat, the January ice bitter by the buried, hands forced into his pockets, and his hood pulled around his face. Micah must have heard me, because he glanced my way, startled, grief written on his face. And then his expression changed.

He stepped toward me, his expression full of something like hope.

"Daniel?" he said. "Is Chris okay? No one will let me see him."

He stopped walking when I didn't reach out for him and looked at me uncertainly.

"His leg is gone, down from his knee," I explained dispassionately, and then touched my face, "and his burns are bad, the left side of his face from his temple to his chin."

"Shit. Shit." Micah bent at the waist, as if he couldn't breathe, and he was crying.

"How is it you don't have a mark on you?" I asked, still eerily calm, and utterly focused.

He took his hand from his pocket, and pulled up his sleeve, exposing bandages. "I was burned," he began. He dropped his hand when I didn't comment, forced it back into his pocket, wincing as he did so.

I imagined the burn hurt a little, maybe even a lot, but he was there, as whole and real as when he'd left my bed on that terrible day.

In my mind I saw Chris in the hospital, the covers raised over the cage which protected his surgical site, then dipping lower where his ankle should have been. I saw a clear image of Isaac the day before he died, knocking for Chris and grinning at me as if he had the greatest secret to tell his best friend.

And here was Micah, telling me he had slight burns on his arm? The same man who'd told me in one breath that he loved me and then had stolen my car, driving it into a bridge and killing one boy, leaving another maimed and in a coma.

My fist flew, clenched aggression targeting Micah's face, his cheekbone, and I heard a satisfying crunch. He staggered back a step, but he didn't go down, and he didn't take his hands from his pockets. I was too fast. I hit him again, blood flecking his face, dissipating into the icy air. He moved again, the force of my blows shoving him back.

Still, his hands remained in his pockets, and he was unnervingly quiet, taking my hits as if they were nothing at all. Another punch connected with his lip and split the skin, and this time he grunted in pain. He staggered backward toward the next grave and bent back over the stone marker with the force of that final blow. I stepped closer. I hit him again, connecting with his jaw, but the hit wasn't hard. There was nothing to it; he didn't move away.

"You took my car," I yelled, right in his face.

"You said I could borrow it," he pleaded.

I raised my hand to hit him again, but he winced, and closed his eyes, and I wanted him to look at me. "Open your damn eyes!"

He did, and he wouldn't avert his gaze, naked grief in his expression.

"Daniel, please listen."

"You've destroyed Chris' life."

"I know."

"You need to leave Whisper Ridge, and never come back. I don't want to see your face, I don't want Chris to ever see you again. You understand?"

"I understand," his tone low and broken.

"You will never come back here." I shook him. He was smaller than me, thinner, lighter, and I shook him so hard his head snapped back. "Promise me!"

"I pr—promise," he said through tears.

I was disgusted by him, hated him, wanted to kill him right there on Isaac's grave.

"I hope they lock you up and throw away the fucking key!" I was still shouting, and he didn't move, just stared at me with those pale eyes, red and wet from crying. He wouldn't stop crying. "Don't fucking stare at me!"

I shoved him one last time, and then before I could work out what the hell I was still doing there shouting at him, I pivoted and turned my back on him, and on Isaac's grave, and the entire carnage.

2
MICAH

Nine years later

RACHEL DROPPED THE GUN, her hands shaking.

The kid screamed behind her, bashing his tiny fists against his head. The sound piercing in the silence after the gunshot, and I wanted him to stop screaming just so I could think.

Fear and indecision paralyzed me, adrenaline making me shaky. What the hell had my little sister done? What had *we* done? I stared at the gun, and the blood that splattered the wall behind her husband and pooled under his lifeless body.

"He was trying to kill us," she sobbed, and fell to her knees, grabbing her son and holding him close. I had to think on my feet.

"Fuck. I don't know what to do—we need to call the cops." I pulled out my phone.

"No, please, the local cops, they know what's here, they know what happens. He was my husband…"

"Jesus." I catalogued the chaos I'd walked into. The compound for the Brothers of Chiron, the blood, and the drugs, and the gun. There were figures in the shadows watching us, but no one stepped forward to help. It was as if I'd walked onto a movie set, and nothing was real. She scrambled to stand and tugged at my arm with a strength that belied her size, let alone the fact she was pregnant.

"Please, before they kill us," she pleaded and tried to drag me away from the shadows in the dark and the blood on the floor.

I stared into her pale eyes, so like my own, and I was thrust back to a time when it was the two of us against the world. I would do anything for my sister, and by extension my nephew, who'd stopped crying and now stared at me in absolute silence. He was looking to me to fix this, but how could I fix the fact his daddy was dead at my feet?

"Fuck. Rachel?" I wanted a solution, one that made sense, but Rachel just stared at me with panic in her eyes, and blood on her hands from when she'd checked his pulse.

"We have to go," she said.

Gently, I eased the gun out of her hands and pushed it into my pocket. She sobbed, incapable of any more words. I should stay, talk this out with the cops. They'd understand she was protecting her son, that she was in a dire situation.

There's no proof that it was self-defense. And you have a record, you fucking idiot.

"I had no choice, please, Micah, you have to believe me."

Wait, she was asking me what I thought of her? "Of course, I believe you, I was here, he had a gun to the kid, but now, shit Rachel, I don't know what to do."

"We need to go."

"No, we should call the cops—"

She pointed at the shadows, the men standing in the dark, staring at us, the woman next to them, the two small children.

"They'll kill me—"

"We can't just go—"

She shoved me back toward the car. "Then I'll stay, you go, but please take Laurie—"

"No, Mom, no." Little Laurie held his mom tight and shouted the words.

I heard them both. She wanted to stay and face the wrath of the rest of them? Willing to have the cops arrest her? And she wanted me to take her son, my nephew, to wait around for them, happy to have them take her away? The people watching weren't stopping her going, but one of them stepped closer, a rifle in his hand. They'd kill her, I didn't have to know the place to know they weren't ever going to let her go again.

"I'm not leaving without you. The baby…what will they do to your baby when it's born?" I couldn't begin to think of the horrors of leaving my sister and a newborn. I made a decision I might one day regret, but it was the only one I could make.

Indecision turned to my own kind of fear. What I'd seen tonight, what I'd heard… I had no choice. I had to get my small family away from there. I couldn't stay, not if they were coming after us. I only had to check out my sister's expression, she wasn't just afraid, she was terrified, and I could hear Laurie sobbing again.

"Momma," Laurie sobbed.

"Get in the car," I said.

Rachel scooped Laurie up and stumbled to the car at the end of the path. She scrambled awkwardly into the back and held Laurie close, and with one last look at the scene, and the shadowy figures that moved closer, I followed. Rachel tried to calm Laurie.

"I won't let them hurt you, I promise."

God, it sounded like the kind of thing she used to say to me.

The snow was heavier now, a persistent swirl of white around us. I got back in my car. They could come after us but first, I would get my sister and her kids to a safe place, where people knew them and could watch over them. I took the gun from my pocket, and held it, examined it briefly, squeezed my fingers on the barrel and the stock. Then I shoved it back again and started the car.

Even though I'd promised the man I'd once loved that I would never return, even though he said he would kill me if he ever saw me again. I had to take what was left of my family home.

Back to Whisper Ridge.

3

MICAH

LAURIE HAD FALLEN ASLEEP IN THE BACK AND RACHEL was as still as stone in the passenger seat. At first, she was quiet, then she cried, and then she was quiet again. I didn't know what to say to her.

"What did I do?" she began to sob again.

I wanted to have the answer. I think she maybe expected me to know what to say, but I was coming up empty.

The rest of the journey was done in silence; five hours was all it took to take us from the fire to the cool safety of our childhood home.

We stopped once for the bathroom and I checked my phone for any news of what had happened. Of course, there was nothing, but it had only been an hour. Then it hit me that I could be tracked to where we were through my phone and I considered dumping it. But what good would that do? The damage had been done, so I pocketed it and tried not to worry.

I didn't have a handbook on how to run from a murder,

or on rescuing my sister from a cult. I bet page one would warn me *not to take a phone that could provide a way to track me.*

We reached Collier Springs a little after two in the morning, the darkness absolute in the empty ranch lands between the town and Whisper Ridge, where we'd grown up. Only twenty minutes away and already my stomach was in knots. As we drove through town I expected ghosts to rear up and drag me from the car.

Or Daniel. What would Daniel think of my coming back after I promised him I wouldn't? My nineteen-year-old self had deeply loved him, and I know he'd hated me when I'd left town. Would nine years have provided enough space for things to change? I could close my eyes and see him; his dark hair, deep brown eyes, his smile, the cockiness in his walk, the way he made love to me, the kisses.

As soon as we hit the road to the Lennox Ranch my memories of a long-lost love vanished, and I was running through the reasons why I'd come here, instead of running for Mexico. Maybe going south was an option, or possibly we could try to get over the border into Canada. We just needed somewhere to stop. We pulled up outside the house and killed the engine.

"I don't want to go in," Rachel murmured, as we sat in the car outside the old place. There were no lights inside, but the porch light came on. I knew what she meant about not wanting to go in. We'd both left this place for different reasons, but somehow, we'd ended right back where everything had started. She reached for my hand and I laced my fingers with hers. I felt like the big brother who used to hold his sister's hand when he was only a kid himself, trying to give comfort.

Laurie stirred in the back and Rachel glanced back at her son.

"What do I do? Micah?"

She was looking to *me* for answers?

I released my fingers from her hold and got out of the car, going to the back door and lifting a sleepy Laurie, holding him close. He roused, glanced up at me sleepily, and squirmed to be let down. Rachel stroked his hair.

"It's okay Laurie, Uncle Micah is looking after us." He relaxed, but kept his eyes firmly fixed on Rachel. The snow was deep, and she was only in cheap tennis shoes, her coat old, her legs bare under fabric that was probably a dress or skirt. She had to be freezing and we needed to get inside. Laurie was buried deep in my coat and some blankets I had in the truck but he shivered as the cold hit him.

"Let's go."

Rachel made her way through the snow by my side, awkwardly, her hands shaking, her face grim, but she was the one who knocked soundly on the door.

A light went on inside the house. What the hell would Amy and Jeff think, us turning up in the middle of the night?

The door was cautiously opened, a woman's face appearing in the crack. Aunt Amy appeared older than I knew her to be, a robe wrapped around her, as she blinked onto the lamp-lit porch and let out a soft gasp.

She widened the door, seemed to assess Rachel, her baby bump and the child in my arms, and ushered Rachel inside, leaving me to follow with Laurie at a distance until I stood inside the small mud room.

"What's the fuss?" Jeff called from somewhere in the house.

"You need to come out here," Amy said, and closed the door behind me.

Her husband ambled into the main room, a rifle in his arm. I moved protectively between Rachel and him.

He lowered it as soon as he realized who it was, but he took the time to peer out of the window as if he was expecting trouble to be following, before locking the front door. Probably against any unforeseen problems that I could have brought with me. He and I hadn't exactly parted on good terms nine years before and I didn't imagine we'd be much in the way of friends now.

He'd wanted me to be a man, to stay and work the ranch.

But I'd made a promise to go.

"Coffee?" Amy asked, and helped Rachel sit at the table. Jeff made coffee, all the time staring at me balefully, and muttering under his breath. He wasn't as ornery way back, the way I recalled him, but he seemed to be treating our arrival as if it was some personal slight.

He'd probably never expected to see me again.

You and me both.

I wasn't sure what to do with Laurie. It wasn't right to take him to one of the old bedrooms, he'd wake up and need his mom, so I laid him on the sofa and pulled a blanket over him. He looked so much like the pictures of me as a kid, all blond hair I thought had never been cut, it was long and all around his face. From what I'd seen, he hid behind it a lot. He was thin and pale and when I brushed his hair back I could see bruises on his left temple. I kept my cursing internal, and stood to see Amy watching my every move.

"I'm not hurting him," I defended myself immediately.

Amy's lips thinned but Rachel's expression softened. "Of course, you're not."

"Sit yourself down, both of you," Amy interrupted and then indicated the chair she'd put coffee in front of. I did as I was told. The coffee was hot, and the sandwiches she'd made thick with peanut butter. I wasn't hungry, but I ate, which was more than Rachel did. She was crying again and rocking a little. I shuffled my chair closer to her and patted her back, which was the extent of my support capabilities. The last thing I needed was for her to blurt out what had happened and have Amy or Jeff call the sheriff up here to tell them the awful story. I needed time to make Rachel see this had to stay a secret, but I could see the guilt in those tears, hand in hand with shock.

I hated this room, and my sister's tears just made it worse. I remembered her crying in here, over Mom dying, over my dad raising his hands to her. I remembered the fights. Way too many memories of bad times had slid into these walls and made them close in on me whenever I'd stepped inside as a kid. They were still here, those memories, along with the stench of alcohol, and the air of death that was in every part of them. I bet Rachel remembered the same things and that couldn't have helped.

Stay quiet, Rachel, keep it all in. Keep it to yourself. Let me deal with everything.

"Do we need to call the sheriff?" Amy asked, gesturing

at Laurie who was turning in his sleep and snuggling down into my coat.

"No," I said. Maybe I sounded defensive, I don't know, but her steely eyed gaze narrowed on me, heavy with accusation.

"What did you do?"

I wasn't even going to give that the courtesy of a reply. It had always been about what I'd done, nothing changed.

"There's no place for you here," she stated simply, "But Rachel and the boy can take her old room."

I didn't ask what was in my old room. There was no way I was going back there, I'd die with the onrush of reminders in that small space. Maybe Amy had made it into a sewing room, or something equally final.

"You should sleep," I said to Rachel, but she shook her head. I didn't want to argue, but I could see hysteria in her eyes, and she was close to losing control. I helped her to stand, carried Laurie, and walked her to the old bedroom. Laurie looked up, his expression frighteningly empty. Had he gone into shock? Should I have been doing something for that? Getting a doctor? Making him a drink? Who the fuck knew.

I knew nothing about how to help him forget the death he'd seen tonight.

Glancing into my old room as we passed, I saw it was empty. No bed, no drapes at the windows. Nothing. Amy had wiped the house clean of me. I hadn't really expected anything else. They were happy enough to take my money but wanted nothing to do with me as a person.

Talking of which, the money I had sent them didn't seem to have gone far in fixing up the house, so I guess it had all gone to the land. I'd see better tomorrow.

When I went back into the kitchen there was no sign of Amy, but Jeff was there, unlocking the door.

"You're not welcome." He indicated the cold outside.

Like I don't already know that.

I shrugged, as if it meant nothing, and to be honest, right then not a lot meant anything to me. My car was the only option. Belatedly I realized my coat was still on the sofa and I turned back to get it. Jeff had thrown it out the door, into the snow, along with the blankets I'd wrapped Laurie in. *Well shit.*

I couldn't be bothered to muster my anger, to put Jeff in his place, and I needed to get myself somewhere warm. I pushed my way back into the house and sat on the sofa in the dark.

I slept, but it was just a mess of nightmares. I dreamed of flames and guilt and madness and woke to a wicked cold in my bones. I'd experienced worse but that didn't mean it was easy.

Dawn was blue and mauve, and there had been more snow in the few hours I'd managed to sleep. Everywhere was utterly still. I made coffee, waiting for Amy or Jeff to jump out and tell me I couldn't. Then thought up a list of things I needed to do.

Get Rachel to a doctor. I think. At least, that was the right thing to do. I checked on her, but she was fast asleep, Laurie cuddled into her side. She was frighteningly pale, her hair matted, and she gripped Laurie tight even in her sleep. As I turned to leave she called after me, just my name, so low I almost didn't hear it.

I turned back to her and waited for her to say more, but she simply stared at me.

I reached over, tugged blankets around her and pressed a soft kiss to her forehead.

"I'm going out for a walk, go back to sleep, you'll be okay here."

She closed her eyes and gave a short nod. Then, fueled with coffee and stolen cookies I walked some of the ranch.

I followed the path down the incline from the house, noting the fences worn and broken in places, at the irrigation channel blocked by debris, at the fallen trees on the far side of the land, and the absence of animals. I knew that the Lennox Ranch kept minimal livestock now, horses, there were stables, I knew all this because Aunt Amy sent reports on an annual basis to my inbox, and by return I sent every cent I could to keep the place alive.

If the money wasn't fixing the house, or supporting livestock, or fixing the ranch, where the hell had it gone?

Sending money was the only way I knew to keep the ranch ready for Rachel and any family she had. I hadn't even known if she'd had family. I guess, the land would belong to little Laurie one day, along with my sister's unborn child. This was my birthright, and I was the sixth generation Lennox who could call this place theirs. Not a single part of this belonged to Rachel, some stupid throwback to male inheritance, but I had already signed everything over to her in my will.

Subsidence on the path had taken a huge chunk out of the hill and there was bound to be a mess of debris under the snow. It wasn't easy for a rancher to prevent rock slides, growing up here I had learned to work with Mother Nature, not against her. But the fall had destroyed some of the path and it needed to be rebuilt.

My ranching heart ached to see the mess. For all his

drinking, Dad had had a handle on things, running the ranch with two extra hands, along with me. I had loved this land once.

And then Mom had died. I'd been ten years old, and my life changed forever.

I kicked at a stone and it tumbled ahead of me on the path. I stooped to pick it up, tossing it in my hand and staring out over Lennox land.

My future had been tied to these acres until I'd had to leave. I threw the stone as far as I could, and it arced high in the sky, falling to earth a long distance away. My arm had always been good, not as good as my best friend Chris's. He'd actually been scouted for pro-ball, and would have gone all the way with his tenacity and skill but for one stupid night where I'd fucked everything up.

Grief consumed me and I crouched down, struggling to breathe properly. I didn't usually allow myself to reflect on Chris, or Isaac, or the night I'd broken everything. But here, on Lennox land, all I could think about was the boys I'd known, and all the possibilities I'd destroyed. Only when I could get my thoughts back into the box I locked them in, was I even able to walk again.

When I got back to the ranch everyone was awake.

"I'm going into town," Jeff announced, as if he couldn't bear to be in the same room as me, and Amy pursed her lips as she watched him go.

"We need to get this one to a doctor," she said and nodded at Rachel.

"No doctor," Rachel said immediately. She looked at me for support but I wasn't going to give that. She was ashen, exhausted, and the way she was rubbing her back, something wasn't right.

"If you need to," I said, and she winced.

"They'll know," she said, so softly I had to strain to hear.

"Know what?" Amy leaned forward, clearly worried she was missing out on something.

"Nothing," I said, and I stared at Rachel with warning in my eyes.

She stared back at me with a defiant tilt to her chin. God, she'd been stubborn as a kid, using the fact that she was younger than me to great effect, and she wasn't going to be told. "I'm fine. Tired is all. I'm going to get some sleep, if you'll keep an eye on Laurie."

Amy nodded. "Of course, I will."

"I meant Micah," she explained. Amy's eyes widened — she was shocked, but not as much as me. I worked with kids on the job I'd just left, but they'd been at the ranch for lessons. I wasn't going to argue though, because I believed Rachel was protecting herself. Amy's wasn't the warmest welcome we'd had, and maybe we were reverting to type, the siblings who let no one else in. There was very little warmth in that realization; we'd stayed insular for survival —that was all.

"I can do that," I said. "We'll visit with the horses," I said, daring Amy to argue. Laurie and Rachel, heads together, seemed to come to a mutual decision, and she helped him pull on his coat and all his cold weather extras. He looked somber and kissed his mom, and then her belly. I wished I could've heard what they were saying but this was mom and son time. He studied me warily, but when Rachel whispered something to him he lifted his arms to be picked up.

When we left, I skirted the farm house, came into the

yard via the tired looking stables and stopped for a while to visit with the horses. There were four, and they were well cared for. That much was obvious. I knew that two of them were stabled there by clients. The other two belonged to the ranch, replacements for my long-gone horse Charlie-Blue.

"What ya doing in here, boy?"

Jeff leaned on a shovel with a suspicious look on his face. The guilty part of me wanted to scurry away and hide, but I was a Lennox and this was my place. Then Jeff saw Laurie and his expression softened a little.

"We're here to see the horses," I said, and Laurie slid down to hide behind my legs. There was a flicker of compassion on Jeff's face.

"Don't you go messing with them," he finished in a gruff voice and left, calling over his shoulder. "I'm going to town. You think your sister needs anything?"

I shrugged. What did a pregnant woman need? I'd have liked to have said for Jeff to bring back a doctor but after Rachel's conviction that she just needed sleep, who was I to say that wasn't okay? This was her body, her baby.

I just worried she was in shock and I would miss something vital.

Should I just take over? Make decisions for her?

We spent a long while with the horses, Laurie asking questions in a soft voice, but not getting too close. It wasn't that he was afraid of them, just respectful of their size. We had some lunch and then Laurie began to yawn, so I took him, and some food and coffee, to Rachel, and left them to nap. She looked better, her skin not quite as pale, but her eyes were so full of grief it broke my heart.

I went back out to the barn, and moved bales and boxes

to one side, daring Jeff to tell me I couldn't, and finally got to what I wanted, the door to the old bunkhouse. It had been part of the barn since the first Lennox decided it made sense for the hands to be as close to the animals as possible. Just off of there was a room that dad had partitioned for me and Rachel when we were kids. A place to get us out of Mom's hair. Faded paint on the wall was all that remained of a mural Rachel had painted. Back when Dad was caring, he'd boarded the small space and added a door. No heating, but the room was good enough to sleep in and out of the snow. I went into the house, found blankets, and made up the best bed I could before stacking bales of hay around the sides for insulation.

Then I sat and checked the news on my phone for the tenth time that day.

Still no reported news about a murder. Is that a good or a bad thing? Part of me wanted us to be found out, for the matter to be dealt with. Get arrested, make things right, cite self-defense, tell someone what kind of shit was going down in that place. The other part of me was relieved we'd made it through so far without garnering attention. If they followed Rachel, if they wanted to arrest her I wasn't sure I could've handled that. She shouldn't have to go through any more.

I won't let her go through anymore.

Tomorrow I could go a couple of towns over and buy a camp bed, and some heaters, but for today there was only one thing I wanted to do.

Visit Isaac.

4

DANIEL

"YOUR BROTHER'S HERE," CHLOE WINDHAM DECLARED. Her knock, announcement, and charging into my room happened simultaneously and I jumped back in my chair.

"Which one?" I asked, and straightened the chair, cursing under my breath as it snagged on the radiator. I sat back down and straightened papers. No way was I going to look up at Chloe because I knew exactly the expression she'd be using. The one that conveyed pity and worry and was a step away from coming around my desk to give me a hug. People didn't hang around to talk to me when I was rude to them, so rude was my default setting. Pity, worry and hugs were the three things I didn't need today.

I'd seen the article this morning, another interview from one of my colleagues on the six-month anniversary of the hostage situation. I remembered the colleague, Zach, he was an administrator, a ballbuster, kept the ER docs in line, and he'd been the one to speak to the gunman first. At that point I hadn't even known there was a shooter in the building. Hell, nothing much filtered through to the chaos in the back rooms where we tried to save people's lives.

In an apparent need to punish myself, I read the article from beginning to end. I didn't need reminding, but it grounded me to remember there was a reason for some of the insane things going through my head.

But I bet one of my brothers had seen it and felt I needed to be checked on. I wanted to curl under my desk to avoid any more shit.

"Which one?" I repeated, with that tone I'd been using, the one that stopped discussion and sympathy dead on its feet. I immediately discounted Mark, he was away at college. So, it could either be Chris, who'd want to try to get me talk to him, or Scott who'd be wanting to report on some new investment opportunity.

Neither of those options filled me with any enthusiasm. I didn't want to talk to Chris yet. Since coming home from Charlotte, I'd successfully managed to evade getting too deep into the drama of the car accident that had taken his leg nine years ago. I deliberately didn't spend much time at my parents' place and when I did, I changed the subject.

Now I was home full-time, and had been for two months, I couldn't avoid *the talk* with my brother for much longer. God help me if it was Chris cornering me at work to talk about my feelings.

And Scott? Well, I'd already invested as much capital as I could afford in his business. I steeled myself for a confrontation, which was the only way I could handle any kind of family meet-up these days.

"It's Scott." She slipped papers onto my desk and I glanced over at the latest patient files. Anything not to have to look at her. I was relieved it was Scott, him I could tell that I had no extra money left, and to get lost so I didn't lose control of my tightly wound emotions.

"I'm busy."

"He says he'll wait, shall I get him to wait outside?"

Why? Is him waiting going to make this any less excruciating when he does come in here?

"No, I guess you can send him in, and can you get this off to the lab" I handed over the vials for blood-work from my last patient, all tidy in their sealed plastic bag. At that point I didn't have any choice. I had to look up because I was getting labelled as being more fragile than rude. I know this, because I overheard Chloe and her daughter talking about it in the clinic kitchen.

Poor Doctor Sheridan.

Chloe was part of the furniture; she'd started working for my dad back when he'd set up practice in Whisper Ridge, and she'd probably outlive me. Her skin was smooth and unlined, her hair perfectly blonde, and if I didn't know she'd just passed sixty, I would've put her at being forty. Good genes, my dad would say, voodoo was mine and my brother's opinion, and my mom would sniff and mutter something about plastic surgery.

I was right though, she did have *that* expression on her face that could be summed up in one word. Compassion. Working with the woman who, at one point in my life, had changed my diapers was like having a family member staring down at me.

"Is that all?" I was rude and to the point, close to losing my cool, and hoping that her going might give me some breathing time.

"Yes, doctor," she inclined her head and went out of the door, leaving it ajar for Scott to come in. No doubt he was out there chatting to Bessie, Chloe's daughter. With the same eerily youthful looks and ash blonde hair, she'd clearly inherited the Windham genes. Scott was all over her, but that could be more because she was searching for a place to buy in Whisper Ridge to settle, and less about flirting with her.

I heard him before I saw him, his voice echoing in the old building with its high ceilings. I braced myself, because a visit from a sibling was never a good thing. No one came to my new office to shoot the breeze or take me out for lunch. No, there was either a purpose that benefited them, or it was serious nonsense about reporters, or what was in the news, or something they'd read.

So, I'd come home to Whisper Ridge a few years earlier than planned. Ok, I'd nearly died in the workplace… but I was handling it the best I could, and wished they'd stop pussyfooting around me.

Scott came in cautiously, peeking around the corner. Likely it was self-preservation, seeing as how last time he'd visited, getting all emotional after seeing a news report that featured a photo of me front and center, I'd thrown a stapler at him.

"Hey." He eased his way in fully. He was dressed to impress, his suit sharp, his hair slick, his aftershave wafting in with the warm air circulating the place. He put me to shame. I was in a suit, yes, but I'd long since removed my tie because it choked me, and my jacket was over the back of my chair, replaced by my favorite, faded, college sweatshirt.

I was a doctor, patients didn't come to see me in a suit, they came for help with whatever ailed them. I could've been dressed in a gorilla costume and it wouldn't have mattered. My dad didn't agree, always impeccably turned out in a three-piece suit, but I was a child of the new millennium and I set my own rules. It wasn't so much a rebellion, as the need to be comfortable in case I had one of my panic attacks. At least they'd lessened now, but I was still hyper-aware of things around me, and a tie was like a noose.

"Hey," I leaned back in my chair and waited for whatever he wanted. Only he didn't immediately jump in with anything at all. He'd been laughing out in reception, but in my office, he was deathly quiet. "What's wrong?"

Everyone needed something from me. They needed me to smile. To be happy. To be thankful I was alive.

Easier said than done.

Scott looked at the door, and moved from foot to foot, something he only did when he was anxious.

And then Michelle arrived, the middle Sheridan sibling, and the only girl, out of breath, apologizing for being late.

Shit. What was wrong? Was this some kind of intervention? Last thing I needed was my family pushing me to talk to them. I'd been expecting some kind of family chat in which they all stood in a circle and told me I was a cold, isolated, miserable bastard who needed to get my head out of my ass.

It hadn't happened yet. But, give it time.

With Michelle and Scott there, only Chris and Mark were missing and then we'd have all five Sheridan siblings in one place.

Chris wouldn't be there because he would be teaching at this time of day, and Mark was away at college, so fuck, if they had also turned up then I could safely say that shit really had hit the fan.

And then it struck me. Was this about something other than me? Were Mom and Dad okay? Was Chris okay?

“What?” I asked, abruptly concerned. Michelle closed the door and then sat in the patient chair. Scott hovered behind her. They exchanged looks and I was just about done with people worrying what to say in front of me. Either skulking around me, or blatantly asking me if I was okay and did I need anything. Why didn’t people treat me normally? Like the eldest of the five Sheridan kids, or like the trained and experienced doctor I was, with years of education and emergency room experience under my belt? Why were they all determined to stick me in a box labelled *victim* and try to protect me from everything? Just as I’d worked myself up a full head of steam, Scott said.

“I saw Jeff this morning.”

“Jeff who?” I knew quite a few Jeffs in town and at Collier Springs hospital where I worked a few shifts each week on outreach support.

“Jeff from up at the Lennox place, Jeff Reynolds, and I asked him, casually, whether there was any news on my proposal for buying the land. He was squirrelly and wouldn’t look at me. Then he did a sharp turn and started to walk the other way, so I followed him and asked him if everything was okay.”

He seemed to run out of things to say; this from the brother who could talk the hind legs off a donkey.

He was the salesman in the family, wheeling and dealing in property and land with his own real estate business covering Whisper Ridge and the towns around. I knew he was sniffing up at the Lennox place because that was some prime land and he'd said he had two developers wanting to turn part of it into some kind of housing. Not that this was going down well with the locals. No one wanted housing with city types messing up the place. Least of all me. I might have spent a lot of years in the city, but Whisper Ridge was in my heart and I didn't want anything to change. Not only that but the Lennox Ranch held some nightmare memories that I didn't want to think about today.

"Wait, so this isn't about Mom?"

"No."

"Or Dad?"

"No, look, listen a minute."

"Is it Chris? Is he okay?"

"Shit, Daniel, can you just listen for fuck's sake?" Scott snapped, and then looked instantly contrite. Fuck my family and their reticence to expose any kind of raw emotion to their poor fucked-up brother.

"Then get on with it." I prompted.

Michelle wouldn't meet my eye and that freaked me out as well. As the middle of the five siblings she was sass and fire and peacemaker all rolled into one. But now she rubbed her belly where the first of the Sheridan grandchildren was biding its time with only a few weeks left in her pregnancy.

"Jeff said something," Scott said. He gripped the back of Michelle's chair until his knuckles whitened.

"Jesus," I snapped. My usual patience with anyone was long gone. "Just spit it out already."

Scott blanched. "We don't know how you'll react—"

I reared up from my seat and planted my fists on the desk. "I'm not some delicate freaking flower and if you don't stop tiptoeing around me like I'm damaged goods and likely to explode at a moment's notice, then I will come over there and beat the living shit out of you. I'm still your big brother and I will take you down."

Scott held up a hand, a flash of something in his eyes. I expected him to give me some explanation of how there was no way I could take him now he was taller than me, but he didn't. This was clearly not the time for sibling rivalries, but anger prevailed.

"You *are* a delicate freaking flower!" Scott shouted, before realizing where he was, and lowering his voice. "You're on edge all the time, and no one can say a word to you."

"Fuck you Scott, back in Charlotte—"

"Don't go there, not unless you tell us everything."

I stopped myself from shutting down. I couldn't handle the *everything* part of that sentence, and my silence gave Scott time to carry on with whatever he'd come to tell me.

"Rachel's back," he said, finally.

That was it? I made a quick connection in my head between Jeff Reynolds and a Rachel. There could be only one connection really.

"Rachel Lennox?" I waited for the nod. What other Rachel would be messing with my brother's head? Or cause my heavily pregnant sister to drag herself out in the frigid February air? "So?"

"She's not alone," Michelle finished, when Scott evidently had run out of things to say.

"Cut to the chase, guys." So, she was with someone, husband, boyfriend? The fact that she'd come to visit Whisper Ridge was something in itself; she'd left at eighteen to go to college and never looked back, but something was going on here. That thing had to be bad to strike Scott dumb and, with dread, I began to make connections. "What the fuck is going on here?"

Scott stepped away from the chair, stood between me and the door and planted his feet.

"Micah's here."

One name was enough to shake the foundations of my soul. I was around the desk and heading for the door in a second, a need to get out of the building burning inside me. I only stopped when Scott became a brick wall blocking my exit.

"Wait, Daniel, don't go up there half-cocked—"

"I'm not going to him, I just need… Get the hell out of my way," I snapped, my chest tight, and shoved at my not-so-small little brother. Scott took the shove, rocked back on his heels, but didn't move.

"Calm down, Danny," he said, and held up his hands. I tried to sidestep him, dread making the world around me dark with temper, and the urge to run, front and center.

"He said he'd never come back," I snapped, all rational thought escaping me in a rush. I shoved at Scott again, but this time he stepped back until he leaned on the door; there wouldn't be any way past him.

"We know," Michelle said, and I half turned, seeing her right there at my side. She was crying, big fat tears that rolled down her face and collected on her thick sweater.

All the pressure left me, and I knew I'd been played. Scott had come to tell me this shit, but he knew that Michelle, and my nearly-there niece or nephew would be enough to diffuse the instant anger or panic symptoms. I backed away from Scott, leaned against my desk and scrubbed my eyes with my fists, then spent a while settling my breathing.

"What the hell is he doing here?" I spat the words out at Scott as an accusation more than an observation.

"Daniel," Michelle murmured in that tone that always cut through me. "Don't."

I didn't know what to do. I had patients to see. I had grief in my heart, panic gripping my chest, and PTSD symptoms crawling inside me like ants. I couldn't breathe and felt my way around the desk to my chair.

"I have work." I waited for them to leave.

Michelle leaned over and patted my hand.

Just leave.

"Are you okay?" she asked, gently.

"Leave," I said, and wished for once my siblings would actually listen to me. She and Scott hovered by the door.

Why won't you both just leave? So I can have a private freak-out instead of you seeing all the horrible, black, cancerous parts of me.

"You gonna kill Micah if you see him?" Scott asked, arms crossed over his chest.

"What?" I was too lost in the shock of hearing that Micah was anywhere near Whisper Ridge.

Kill Micah? I'd said that I would.

In my cruelest dreams back then, I'd wanted to hurt Micah for what he'd done, put my hands around his throat and choke him.

Then there were the other dreams, the ones I couldn't stop, where all I could see was one perfect summer where I thought I'd been in love.

I'd made a promise nine years ago, I'd said to Micah

that if I ever saw him back in Whisper Ridge again, I would hurt him. Just as I had done at Isaac's fresh grave, I would punch him over and over until the very ends of my fear and guilt were ragged and done.

But I was a doctor now, I did no harm, and my world was different. There could be no more black and white for a man who had seen what I had.

The worst of it was that I'd kept the guilt alive when I'd worked in the ER, because it was my job to save lives however they ended up in my care. There was no time for judgement when my hand was in a gang member's chest trying to find a bullet. Everything there was a mix of grays that I could never fully understand, but which had fundamentally changed me.

And then the ER had been on lockdown and I had been in the middle of a situation that had left me shaken and changed again.

"I won't kill him," I said. "I'm not a murderer, for fuck's sake."

"So, if you see him you'll just talk to him?" Michelle sounded a long way past worried. "You won't confront him and cause issues for Chris?"

Jesus. I hadn't even thought about my brother's reaction to Micah being in town.

Michelle forged ahead. "He's in a good place, Daniel, he doesn't need you fighting Micah."

That question hit me hard, "I just said I won't hurt him. I won't cause trouble for Chris." Then it hit me there was a much deeper question that needed answering. "Fuck, does Chris know he's back?"

Best friends since they were tiny, my brother Chris and the newly returned Micah Lennox had been close. The two of them, and Isaac Jennings, had been joined by an unbreakable bond. They'd grown up together, found trouble wherever they could, had each other's backs more than any friend I had ever had.

Isaac, dead. Chris, an amputee. Micah, alive.

"I don't think Chris knows. Apparently, Micah has only been back since last night," Scott said. He sagged back against the door. Abruptly, he wasn't the guy who worked out, sold property like candy, and could talk his way out of any kind of trouble with confidence. No, this Scott was the one who needed his big brother to take a stand, to be the one in charge of this. He didn't need me to be in the middle of a freaking panic attack. I focused on my breathing, on the desperate need for air, stopped myself clawing at my throat. I turned and stared out of the window, at the mountains, and finally I had some control.

"You need to let *me* tell Chris." I couldn't believe the words that left my mouth. I'd spent so many years circumventing the necessity to talk about the accident with my brother. What was I doing saying I would talk to him?

Michelle sighed, "Daniel, you've been avoiding talking to Chris about the accident since you came home—"

"No, I haven't," I lied. "I'll tell him," I interrupted before Michelle could go full-on understanding and supportive and pull down a little more of the wall I'd erected around my emotions. I was the eldest and Chris needed to hear this from me.

"And you won't do anything stupid to Micah if you see him?" Michelle looked as if she was going to cry again. I could handle most things, but not my sister's tears. She'd been the one who'd bandaged my hands where I had cut them after hitting Micah over and over. Why would she expect anything different from me now?

I caught her gaze. Over the years I'd learned how to lie and appear as if I was being truthful at the same time. She was the sibling who always saw through me, but today I think she was ready to believe every word I said.

"It's been nine years, Michelle, I won't hurt him."

"You blamed him for what happened to Chris," she murmured.

"That was then."

I didn't have hate in my heart anymore for Micah Lennox. Nor did I have compassion or forgiveness.

I had nothing.

No sympathy, or understanding, just a big empty space that held nothing but bad memories. Ones I didn't pull out too often to think on. Any residual empathy I'd felt for Micah had vanished after I'd found Chris in the bathroom with a bottle of pills because he couldn't imagine having a life after losing his leg.

When I'd been in the ER six months ago, with a gun to my temple, it wasn't my life that had flashed before me, it was a whole mess of regrets over the accident, my brother, and the part I'd played in everything. I didn't specifically think about Micah and what we'd meant to each other. But it seemed like ever since that day I hadn't been able to shake the feeling that I should track him down. Maybe we could apologize for what we'd both done. Or, if not to say sorry, then at least to talk about things so that the past could finally be settled.

Was him being in Whisper Ridge my chance to get some peace?

They left, Michelle holding onto Scott's arm, and

throwing one last glance over her shoulder. Scott was back to being jovial and loud with the people and staff in the waiting room—the way he dealt with stress. Michelle was stricken. She didn't need this, not with being so close to having her baby.

I should talk to Chris. Hell, this might've been exactly the right time to clear the air with my brother, and get over the fact that I'd been avoiding the elephant in the room. If Chris even wanted to talk about the things that had happened. And if I could get over the panic I felt every time I had to confront something.

I was the first to admit my head was so full of noise I didn't have room left for real life. I'd lived the last three years working in the emergency room of one of the busiest hospitals in Charlotte, North Carolina. I'd been constantly on high alert there, moving from one crisis to another. Coming back had been *my* choice, but I hadn't managed to leave behind the instinct to go into fight mode as soon as something happened.

My counselor in Charlotte had called it hyperawareness.

The counselor I transferred to here, Devin, said the same thing, and was coaching me on my thought processes. A slow and frustrating process.

I just called it an inability to get my head straight even though I knew what was happening to me.

Doctor, heal thyself.

5

DANIEL

I finished my appointments in a daze, it was just as well the afternoon was slow. As Nana Sheridan used to say, time was going slower than a snail with a cracked shell.

The last appointment was at four, and I had more than enough time to sit at my damn desk and think between patients. I had reports to write, samples to send off, two referral letters, insurance paperwork to complete. I left everything to one side and stared out of the window which faced the fields behind the clinic and with a view up to Whisper Ridge. I could stare at our small part of the Wind River Mountains all day; the *Winds* were my Zen focus where I forgot the mess in my head and concentrated on my breathing. Today, that wasn't working. In fact, nothing was. Not work, not coffee, nor the secret stash of chocolate in my desk which had become my secret comfort, nor the beautiful mountains outside my window.

Micah was back, and my gentle thoughts about finding him and talk hardened as the clock's hands moved. Why was he back? Was he planning on sticking around? He vowed he'd never come home, told me to my face that he agreed he was toxic, that he held all the blame, and that he wasn't coming back to Whisper Ridge after he got out of prison.

I should have known I couldn't trust a nineteen-year-old kid to make a promise he could keep.

I don't know what had happened to him right after prison. I'd heard he moved onto a ranch somewhere, but I didn't care. No one talked about him in the family; he'd gone from being an extra-brother to the five of us Sheridan siblings, to becoming less than nothing.

But I've heard things. That's what happens in small towns like this one; particularly from gossiping patients who'd fall over themselves to hand out morsels of information that they thought I wanted to know. Allegedly, he sent money back to Amy and Jeff at the Lennox Ranch. The way it had been told to me was that it was Micah's extra money that kept the old place going, but I doubted it. Amy and Jeff ran that place from dusk until dawn and kept it going for themselves. And how much could Micah have made as a ranch hand for god's sake? Rumors were that he'd taken to stealing cars, or made his money in other nefarious ways.

I'd heard so many different theories that I'd taken to believing that Micah was as bad inside as everyone said. It didn't matter we'd had a relationship where I'd believed I knew him. He was the man who had hurt my brother, and I'd have believed anything that justified the anger that for so long had bordered on hate.

As for Rachel, she hadn't come back for the trial, had never come back after college, but I hadn't been surprised.

They were close, Micah and Rachel, and even though they'd been driven apart by the cancer that had taken their mom when they were young, Rachel had looked out for her big brother. But, she'd probably been as horrified as the rest of the town at what Micah had done.

Then there was Micah's dad. Edward Lennox had been a big man, dangerous, fond of lashing out at his son and daughter when they stepped out of line. He was gone as well, by his own hand, his wrists cut to shreds, and a final bullet leaving blood and brains on the bathroom wall.

Talk about dysfunctional, the entire family were driven by demons that I couldn't properly understand. No wonder Micah had gone bad, but that didn't excuse him for the one night where he'd destroyed my brother's life.

I'd fallen in love with the bastard, or at least I thought I had. Until everything shattered.

I pulled on my heavy sheepskin coat, looking at the clock. It was a little after four, and I was done with patients, and hell, I needed some air. I locked up my consulting room and strode past reception without saying a word. Chloe called after me, but if I stopped, if she tried to talk to me at that moment I would've lost my shit completely. She had to know something was up, with Scott and Michelle visiting me and then me stalking out of the place as if my ass was on fire.

I bet she was already on the phone to call her son Neil, a county sheriff and someone well versed in the whole Sheridan/Lennox history.

What person in this town wasn't? If I drew a line behind Main Street and the church and curved it back to Whisper Peak, then the south half was Sheridan land, the north was Lennox-owned. Two families, working hard to keep what was theirs, and they'd been pretty amicable most of the time. Hell, Amy Lennox was even supposed to have married my Uncle Liam before he died too young to make any kind of life for himself.

Maybe if that had happened, the great merging of two families, then Christmas Eve 2009 would never have happened.

I reached the end of the road before anyone from the clinic could catch up with me, walking so fast I was only an inch away from running. My breath floated in white clouds in front of my face, and the icy air worked its way into my lungs. After the heat of the Carolinas, I loved the sharp contrast of the ice and snow. I needed that.

A reminder of the person I wanted to find my way back to being.

I pulled my beanie low on my head to stop heat escaping and made the decision to pull out an extra layer of clothes before clinic tomorrow.

"Morning." Josiah Redfern, town mayor and school governor, nodded as he passed, and slowed as if he wanted to stop and talk. I didn't want to talk, so I gave a non-encouraging nod, but kept walking. I was so past worrying about being rude.

I need to get out of here.

A car slowed and crawled alongside me and I didn't even have to look to see who it was. The Sheriff, or as I knew him, just plain old Neil-who-I-once-kissed. God damn Chloe and her network of people who all wanted to mother me.

The old Daniel would have made a joke about how Neil was curb crawling, the new me wasn't interested in starting anything like a conversation with anyone while there was a crushing pressure on my chest.

"Daniel?" Neil called, but I carried on ignoring and the car revved to get my attention.

I slowed my pace a little but wasn't ready to stop.

"A word, Dr. Sheridan?" Neil asked, more than told. He had this way about him, with his drawled country boy vowels and his aww shucks ma'am way of approaching any situation, but under that he was all steel. I liked Neil. He was one of my oldest friends from High School, and we'd had a brief *thing* in the summer after the accident.

The fact he called me Dr. Sheridan made this official and I hated that I resented him with the fire of a thousand suns. I knew why I focused that much hate on him. He must have access to more information about what had happened in Charlotte. Even the bits no one talked about. Every. Fucking. Moment.

I hunched deeper in my coat but didn't stop walking.

"Daniel, come on man," Neil said with a sigh, and then accelerated a little, pulling his truck in front of me and blocking my path. If I'd felt strong and determined I could've pushed my way past, jumped the freaking hood, slid along the length of it, landed dramatically and kept on walking.

But I didn't feel strong.

And the only determination I had in me was to walk off my anger and stress.

I stopped just before I walked into the car and came face-to-face with Neil. He had his arms crossed over his chest and his expression was careful and measured. He certainly wasn't using pity on me, or blatant understanding, or even compassion. He was all about the job at that moment.

"Daniel, I know you've heard that Micah is in town."

"Yep."

"I need a word."

"I don't have time to talk." I had things to do, places to go, hell, people I needed to see. But, mostly I had to walk off the aggression and fear that were acid-hot inside me.

Everything was wrong. What had happened in the Charlotte hospital had destroyed my focus. And even though I'd come to some kind of understanding over Chris's injury all those years ago, the pain of it gripped me when I least expected it.

How could I let any of this go? It was *my* car that Micah had stolen, *my* car that had ended up killing and maiming. And now Micah was back, and I didn't want to see his face, and I had to go to Chris and tell him, and confront a hundred demons from my past.

"Daniel, get into the car," Neil said. "I'll take you home."

The very last thing I needed was to climb into the car with Neil. Our backstory was complicated, and all of it wrapped up with Micah and the accident. I'd used him after Micah left. He'd been the one person I could turn to who wasn't family. He'd seen the way I'd crumbled after the accident. Held me when I'd cried after finding Chris, depressed and trying to kill himself.

He's just seeing nothing has changed with me.

I opened my mouth to argue, but what was the point of explaining any of the mess in my head to another person. No one else needed to know.

"I just have to walk," I said. Why wouldn't people just

leave me the hell alone to work through my issues, instead of getting up in my face all the time?

"We need to talk. Mom said you found out and looked upset."

"Yay, news from the woman who is more effective than fucking CNN," I said. I was joking, using sarcasm, but my tone was brittle, even I could hear that, and Neil's eyes narrowed.

Great. Now I was fucking this up as well. I didn't need to get into some kind of pissed off discussion about Neil's mom being the town grapevine leader. We all knew that to be fact, we all accepted this, and it wasn't a real issue. She was also the town's mother hen, worrying and stressing about us all, and we loved her for it. Maybe I needed Neil to get up in my face and tell me I was an asshole, then he would be treating me like a normal man who dissed his momma.

He didn't make a move to do that, but on the other hand he didn't wave it away either.

"Shit, Neil. I'm sorry," I said, and I meant it.

Neil inclined his head, accepting my lame-ass apology. We stared at each other for a few moments and I could see the calculation on his face. He knew me better than some, but not as much as others. He must've seen me and recalled the kid I'd been, kneeling next to my brother in the dirt and holding his hand as he bled out.

He probably thought he recognized the man I was now, but no one in this town could know the real me.

"Tell me where you're going."

I want to go up to the Lennox Ranch and see for myself that he's back. I want to tell him to leave because he's not welcome here. I don't want to see Chris and tell him Micah is here at the Lennox Ranch.

"I'm just walking," I said out loud.

"Daniel, be honest with me, are you heading up the Lennox place?"

I pulled my hands out of my pockets and held them out, gloved palms up. "No Neil. I'm not walking three miles in this weather; do I look stupid?"

"You want me to answer that?" Neil said, and he smiled, and there was a glimpse of the old Neil there. The one that I'd messed around, the one who'd wanted a future with me and who I'd shoved away as soon as I didn't need him anymore.

The soft smile that reached his dark eyes did me in. It unmanned me and crawled into my head, and those damn tears pricked my eyes again.

No more crying.

"I'm just going up to see Isaac," I finally offered.

He nodded. At some time or another, every person in this town went to Isaac's grave, to visit with the young man who would never get any older than nineteen. Maybe it was to talk, or to remind ourselves of our own mortality, but whatever it was, his grave was a place of sanctuary, somewhere to begin to understand more about ourselves. I needed *that* right now.

"Okay." Neil said. "I'll find out why Micah's here, okay?"

There was that hint of compassion, that insistent implication of him worrying about me, and I refused to accept it.

"We need to get a beer one night," I blurted. "Like we used to."

Like normal friends do.

Neil gave me one of his enigmatic nods. “I’d like that.” He slowly reversed, but I didn’t move until he was back on the road. “Call me if you need me,” he said, and I knew what he was trying to say; Don’t do anything stupid.

“I will,” I reassured. Then, when his tail lights disappeared around the corner I carried on with my walk. I took a left by the boarded-up beauty salon that had once kept a generation of Whisper Ridge women looking lovely, and began the slow climb to the graveyard beyond the tiny church. I wished I’d brought thicker gloves to work. I pushed my hands deeper into my coat and buried my face in my scarf.

I took the long route. The last thing I needed was to talk to anyone from the church, and finally I came to the markers sticking up from the snow, heading instinctively for Isaac’s grave. There was someone there, hunched in their coat, an eerily similar image to the one in my head from all those years ago.

I stopped walking; the unspoken rule here was that if someone was talking to Isaac then that was private business and you didn’t intervene.

But. When the man sighed visibly and turned his face to the sky I knew who it was. Micah.

Blindly, with no thought to what I was doing and with a sharp pain in my heart, I walked around grave markers until I was only a few feet behind him.

If I could get him to leave then I would never have to worry about Chris seeing him again. My job as a big brother would be done. I could reason with Micah. He was still just a man. Right?

And then he must have sensed I was there and as he

turned he pulled back the hood. Micah Lennox. His hair was still as white blond as I remembered, his pale gray eyes wide with shock and then resignation. All of my good intentions vanished, every single thought of *encouraging* Micah to leave, or talking to him rationally, just fled under the weight of my panic.

"You said you'd stay away," I blurted, my hands in fists at my side.

He was saying something to me, but I couldn't hear over the buzzing in my head. In his place was the man who had held me at gunpoint in my ER, the one who had threatened to hurt me and had then killed my friend. The whole mess had been building to that point since I'd come home, it just happened that it was Micah in my way. I stepped forward, my hands in fists.

"I'm sorry, I had to come back for Rachel." There was apology written on his face, and regret. He was asking me silently to understand, but the red mist descended and all I could think about was how Chris would react if he saw Micah.

"You can't be here," I grasped hold of a reason why I was losing control. "If my brother sees you—"

"I had to come back, I didn't have a choice." He held his hands up.

I shouted right in his face, and he didn't flinch. "What the hell are you doing here?" I shoved him. "Standing at the grave of the kid you murdered."

Every messed-up thought that crawled inside my head came out in words of hate full of vitriol.

He paled, and I pushed him again. Then my fist flew like it had done all those years ago. It connected with his mouth and blood trickled from his split lip. His head snapped back and then he grabbed me as I wound up to throw another punch.

He held me close then spoke.

"You want to hit me again? Then go ahead and try, but I'll fight back this time."

He shoved me away, and I stumbled, and for a horrified second all I could do was stare at him.

Then, the panic and pain stilled inside me and I knew what I'd done.

I ran from the graveyard, left Micah where he stood and went straight to the Sheriff's office, my hands by my side, the skin icy. It was a tiny place behind the Whisper Ridge Diner and I found Neil right where I knew he would be, sitting at his desk with files and folders around him.

I sat in his visitor chair and held out my hands, the knuckles of my right-hand scarlet, Micah's blood on them. Neil's eyes widened, but I stopped him talking with a shake of my head.

"He was there. I didn't kill him," I murmured, "but I hit him. Hard."

"Daniel—"

"You need to arrest me."

6

MICAH

I WATCHED DANIEL LEAVE, THEN SLID DOWN TO CROUCH against Isaac's stone. The snow had collected and compressed enough to give me somewhere to sit.

I guess I deserved one punch. I'd promised not to come back, on my sister's life, and Daniel had promised he'd kill me if he saw me again. I was lucky he'd stopped when he had, because I hadn't fought back, but he wouldn't get any second chances to mark me. I was done paying in blood for my crimes. Maybe it would have been a good thing for everyone if Daniel had finished the job and cracked my skull open on Isaac's grave. What was a more fitting end for a man who'd caused so much hurt? At least that way I'd be with Isaac and I could apologize face-to-face.

Not that I believed there was anything after this life I'd fucked up.

But what about Rachel? If I was dead then who would watch out for her if they came after her?

We could have meant everything to each other, me and Daniel. The promise was there for a future I had destroyed.

I deserved his anger. After coming home, I had been expecting some kind of retribution. I just didn't know it would come as fast and hard as it had next to where the boy I'd killed laid at rest. Daniel hadn't seemed right, there had been a manic look in his eyes; not the cold iciness of hate, but the burning intensity of hysterical fear. I knew. I'd seen it in my time behind bars.

But, I couldn't even think about Daniel. My head was too full of what had happened at the compound.

The label of murderer might well have been attached to me for years, but today it was much more.

Yesterday, I'd compounded my sins, watched as my sister killed a man. What would the cops say? I wondered if they'd found the body yet? Or would the people at the compound have hidden what had happened? They refused to have contact with the outside world, but that didn't mean they wouldn't call the cops.

And that would lead them right to Rachel, and eventually to Whisper Ridge.

I still had the damn gun in my pocket, it was heavy and I was fucking stupid for carrying it around with me, but what did I do with it? I'd cleaned off Rachel's prints, as well as I could, and then I held the gun in front of me, in a way that I would've if it were me that had shot the guy who'd tried to stop us. I didn't even have to think about that. If the gun was found, it would be my prints, and it would be me they arrested. That was okay, as long as Rachel and the kids were safe.

If only I'd ever believed she'd want to see me, I would have tracked her down. Not left her at the mercy of the man who'd died.

Rachel's husband.

At some ungodly hour of this morning I had woken with the absolute certainty that I would tell the cops it was me who had shot Callum Prince. Rachel deserved a better deal than the two she'd been handed so far. Hell, Laurie and the baby deserved more. There was no real choice to be made at all.

"Micah Lennox?"

I turned to face the person who knew me, knew my name, and I saw the uniform first. The sheriff. My chest tightened, but along with the instant guilt came a curious sense of peace. Getting arrested would leave no more room for worrying about being found out. I had a fucking gun in my pocket, after all.

Had the people at the commune found the body? Had *they* followed us? Called the law on us? Was this me being arrested?

I took my hands out of my pockets and appeared as unthreatening as someone with a record could. Particularly as the sheriff, who would have access to my records, had his hand resting on his weapon. If he patted me down then I didn't need to worry about anyone calling the cops. I wasn't licensed for a gun, part and parcel of having a record.

"Yes, sir," I said, and then looked past the uniform at the man in it. I recognized him from school, a couple years ahead of me, in Daniel's class if I remembered right. Neil Windham. I remembered his dad, Sheriff Windham, being the one to sit me in a cell the night of the accident nine years ago. He told me I was a murderer, explaining how I would burn in hell for what I'd done to Isaac Jennings, and that someone would kill me in prison. Only that never happened. One year in a cell, trying to be the best person I could be, and I was a free man. So, the elder Windham with all his posturing about right and wrong and everything in between had been inaccurate.

This Sheriff-Windham incarnation observed me steadily, his hands now loose at his sides, snowflakes in his dark hair and his gaze boring into me. At least he'd taken his hand off his sidearm.

"Was hoping you'd still be here, Mr. Lennox. Just had a visit from Daniel Sheridan," he began, and I nodded. Relief flooded me — this wasn't about murder.

Actually, if Daniel had told him where I was, then this was probably some kind of welcome party warning me to leave. "He says he lost control, that there was an *argument*."

I wish I could've said that I felt righteous indignation at this. What had happened wasn't any kind of reciprocal altercation, it was all about Daniel hitting me to get me to leave his fucking perfect-ass town.

"Not really, sir," I answered.

"You're hurt," the sheriff commented and touched his lips, I assume to indicate where he could see blood on my own. Self-consciously I raised a hand and wiped at the spot, looking at my gray glove and seeing the scarlet there. "You'll need stitches," he added.

"I'm okay," I said instinctively. I hadn't gotten stitches the last time Daniel had beaten on me, and I still had a scar up into my hairline to this day. The last thing I needed was to get myself to the clinic where I assume I would find Daniel's father, if he even still practiced medicine.

Why wouldn't he? No one you remember is too old to work. You haven't been away for that long.

The sheriff continued, "Anyways, I came up to find

you, check this out for myself, wanting to know if you're pressing charges against Daniel?"

Wait. I was actually being asked if I wanted to press charges against the man who had every right to punch me? No fucking way. I'd let him get a punch in, but that was my choice and I'd stopped any more.

"No."

He sighed noisily. "Mr. Lennox, you deserve the benefit of justice like everyone else."

"If you say so." I hadn't seen much in the way of people looking past my record, why would the sheriff in Whisper Ridge be anything different? There again, maybe I should have been making nice with local law enforcement, then perhaps they'd take it easier on me for what I'd been part of back at the compound.

Neil stepped closer and I had nowhere to move with Isaac behind me. Strange how I felt completely at peace, and not cornered at all.

"Micah, I want it on the record I don't judge you by what happened nine years ago. You did your time, and what's done is done. The law is there for everyone. You understand what I'm saying?"

He was serious. Maybe he was waiting for me to say something profound, or for me to be filled with gratitude that he was taking a bizarre moral high road.

"Okay," I said, the words a little slurred from the swelling of my split lip.

He hesitated, evidently deciding how to broach the situation. "But, out of interest, how long are you staying here in town?"

Until you find out someone was killed and all the roads lead here. Until everything catches up with us. Until I know for sure my niece or nephew is born, and safe along with Rachel and Laurie.

"I don't know," I gave him, with complete honesty.

He pressed his lips together and then sighed audibly. "If you have any trouble you need to tell me, Mr. Lennox. They're good people in this town, but your arrival hasn't gone unnoticed."

"I know. And I won't have cause to go into town," I said, and pushed my hands into the pockets of my thick coat. "There won't be trouble. But, Rachel, my sister, and her children will be staying, making a life here I think." I met his gaze head on, daring him to tell me she was about as welcome as I was. "I'm staying long enough to get them settled," I added, with the kind of reassurance he appeared to need.

I wondered how long it would be before the death of Callum Prince followed us to Whisper Ridge. A day? A week? Would they ever connect us to him? Would they track down Rachel here and ask questions?

I'll take the blame and turn myself in before they do that.

That was the easy decision to make. Kids needed their momma, and I wasn't letting Rachel be taken away.

I could've told him, about the cult, the compound and the people who'd held Rachel and her son, the ones who had refused to let her go. He could've made it official, and I could've left after he made his protection of her official. But Rachel needed *me*, or at least, at that moment I *needed* Rachel. Anyway, I had to know that the finger of blame was pointing in someone else's direction and not hers for what had happened to the man she'd shot.

"Isaac's mom passed on a few years back, cancer."

"She did?" I didn't know that. I knew that she'd moved away from town to live near her other children after the accident. My lawyer had told me that when he'd said she wouldn't be pushing for a private case against me. He'd given me a letter and it had been read in court. All kinds of things about forgiveness, and that Isaac was just a boy, the same as me.

How she could have that kind of forgiveness in her, I would never know. Isaac had been her youngest child, she'd had him late in life, she'd already been twenty years older than any of our parents. But, even knowing that she would have been in her seventies, it was sad to hear she was gone.

"Please get your face looked at," he told me, and then turned smartly on his heel and walked at a pace out of the graveyard and downward into town.

I left the graveyard, heading uphill and out of the town proper, taking the back path to the ranch house and stopping at the top of the hill. That line, right where the first tiny peak of Whisper Ridge made a soft climb under my feet, was where Sheridan land ended, and where Lennox Ranch began. Turning to look at the town I could see the tops of homes and stores, the neon sign of the gas station with its attached mini-mart. If I focused long enough I could work out which roof belonged to which family. It made me feel uneasy, and I wasn't ready to stare at a place I'd left in my rear-view mirror, so I carried on walking.

Snow swirled around me, the air frigid, but the acres here were beautiful.

Most of the ranch I'd inherited was wide open pasture, crisscrossed with walking paths and animal trails. It used to be that the Lennox Ranch bred horses, and traded cattle; the spread which reached the foot of Whisper Peak and higher was prime cattle land. From there I could see the network of roads that gave access, long dirt and gravel roads, with one remaining cattle guard. There used to be fencing here at the edge of the ranch, but Jeff really had run it into the ground.

Had there even been maintenance of any sort?

The creek wound down from the ridge, snaking past hard rock, digging a path into the soft soil, but it had split since I was last there nine years ago. A rockfall had diverted it and there were several new streamlets that were losing water into the grass. I could see the indentations under the snow, with brittle ice the only indication they were there. Ultimately, the creek wound its way to town, past the bridge and under the road. Under the snow there would be evidence of bushes, and brambles, leaning wood posts, and what was left of barbed wire fences.

If I closed my eyes I could recall riding the perimeter, checking fences with Dad. Last time I remembered that happening I was maybe ten. That had been the year Mom died, and broke our family into tiny pieces. In my memories, there was work being done, hands, horses, cattle, tall trees around the ranch dark green with leaves, and the scent of dust and dirt, as we toiled to make this ranch work. Even in winter there were things we needed to do, and the snow was no obstacle to fixing fences in ground solid with ice.

I crouched down and brushed snow from a bush, the branches brittle with cold, and wondered why the hell I needed to see what was under the snow at all. When I stood, the weight of the gun in my pocket was more than I could handle. I needed to get rid of it, and there was only one place on this ranch where it might never be found.

Jumping the iced creek, I then took a detour behind the ranch house. My jeans were wet through, and even though I'd layered to hell and back, I was still cold. My lip burned where I'd covered it with my scarf and then the blood stuck it there. Just my fucking luck.

One last thing to do.

I found the brick and wood structure, snow banked to one side of it. It was padlocked in four places. I brushed the snow off the nearest lock and shook it, wondering how the hell I was going to pick the lock, but I didn't need to. The wood it was attached to disintegrated at my touch. So much for stopping someone from falling into the ranch well. Below the wood, the well sunk hundreds of feet.

I took out the gun and stared at it for a good minute. I had a hundred scenarios in my head where members of the compound came hunting for Rachel and tried to take her. Would I shoot them? Was I even capable of that?

For my family, yes.

I needed it to go, to be lost as evidence, or for me to use against anyone. I levered up the well cover as best I could under the broken lock, careful not to break any of the others, and then dropped the gun, waiting for the splash, hearing it and dropping the wood back in place.

"What ya doing?" Jeff asked from behind me, and I dropped the lid. Had he seen what I'd thrown in? When I checked his expression, he didn't look suspicious.

"Just noticing this is rotten and needs fixing," I said.

Jeff stared at my face and his mouth dropped open.

"Jeez, boy, what the hell happened to your face?" He sounded shocked, almost worried, and then that slid away.

"Christ, trouble is never far from you is it." He let out a disbelieving harrumph, and straightened up. It seemed to me that he would talk all kinds of bad about me to get my focus off the fact that I could challenge him on the state of the ranch.

Like I can be bothered with that right now.

"Whatever," I said, with no real thought as to the answer I gave. I was too far gone to be thinking about bringing materials back here to fix this. I dragged over a few stones and covered the wood, and all that time Jeff watched me.

"Don't you go meddling around the horses in the barn," he blurted. "Clients won't like you touching the ones we have boarded here. If they leave them, now they know you're back, that is."

"I know my way around horses," I defended. I didn't touch the other comment with a long stick.

"Well we don't need you here messing things up. We've done plenty fine without you here until now."

Jesus, I had so much to say to that, how it was my money that kept this place afloat. How having four horses and a few cows was nothing to be proud of, and how it was my land and I could stand where I damn well wanted.

I said none of it.

"Why isn't the well checked, this is dangerous for kids up here, parents as well."

"No one comes this far up on the land," Jeff said, in a tone that implied I was stupid. "We shut these pastures down a long time ago, rockfall changed the water course, and we didn't have the hands to look after it all. You running off left us in the horseshit."

"I didn't run off," I argued, but he sneered at me and I don't know why I even defended myself.

I inclined my head and strode away from the well and up to the house. It wasn't as if I was any more welcome there, but it was my place, and I wanted to see Rachel and Laurie.

7

MICAH

THE DOOR TO THE HOUSE FLEW OPEN AND LAURIE DARTED out, screaming, a crying Rachel trying to follow.

"Laurie, please!"

I caught the little guy as he went by me, swinging him up into my arms and taking him by surprise. He thumped me and bit me and did everything to get away, but my hold was strong and finally he stopped wriggling but sobbed loudly.

I gestured for Rachel to go inside and shut the door, then I sat on the top step. Awkwardly, I slipped off my coat and wrapped it around him, ignoring the fact my ass was frozen to the wood and that I was shivering hard. Now that the scarf had been yanked from my lip, and I knew it was bleeding again. Then I hugged Laurie as close as I could, stroking his soft hair and whispering that everything was okay, over and over. When he stopped crying his little hands crept around my neck and he buried his face there.

"You want to tell me what happened?"

Laurie shook his head and clung tighter.

"Okay, you don't have to talk."

I think he nodded again, but there was hardly space between his face and my skin, he was so close. "I'm going back in the house, we can find your momma. Is that okay with you?"

"M'okay."

I took him back into the house. Only when I got closer to Rachel, I saw the way she was standing, a hand in the small of her back, and exhaustion lining her face.

"Your face!" she exclaimed and reached for me. I backed away. The last thing I needed was someone I didn't really know anymore touching me.

"I'm okay."

"But, you're bleeding. What happened?"

I ignored the question and instead looked down at Laurie in my arms. He didn't see fit to comment on my face, or the blood, or anything about me in general.

"What happened to spook the little guy?" I asked quietly.

She slumped a little, "He was sitting at the table and he knocked over a jar and it smashed and when that happened…before…" she didn't finish the thought. She didn't need to. From the way Laurie had flown from the house, running from something, I imagined he was scared of being in trouble. What the hell had happened to him back at the compound?

"It's okay," I reassured her, wanting her to know I understood and that she didn't need to explain any more.

"He's just seen so much," Rachel said, and then Laurie stared at me. He reached up and patted my lip and I tried not to wince. That freaking hurt.

"Hey," I said to him, catching his waving hand. I had

an idea brewing about how to focus Laurie. Maybe some of the horse therapy knowledge I had could be used with him? He was my nephew, my blood, was it possible that he could feel the same connection to horses that I had? "Wanna see some horses?" I glanced back at Rachel, asking her silently if that was okay.

She looked at me with such gratitude, her pale eyes bright with tears, and something shifted inside me. Yeah, I carried so much emotional baggage about Dad, and Mom dying, but we were the ones left, and I would do anything she needed me to.

"He hasn't eaten his egg and toast," she said, gesturing at the plate on the table.

I inclined my head to her, indicating she should leave and when she did I placed Laurie on the nearest chair, pushing the toast toward him.

"Food first and then we'll look at horses."

He stared at me with wide eyes, and then he scowled. Hell, I could see myself in him. In the defiant tilt of his head and the little fists he clenched on the table. It seemed as if his despair had turned to temper, just the way his Uncle Micah handled things. I should've told him to eat his food, not to fuss, and to be thankful he had food. Right? Is that what dads did? Because I had no frame of reference from my own dad.

Then I recalled what he'd seen last night, what his dad had looked like dead, and I thought maybe I should be firm and then pull him in for a hug and tell him that everything was going to be okay.

How could I do that second part when I wasn't sure anything in this life *was* okay?

After a short battle of wills, he picked up the toast and

egg and began to nibble on it. He didn't use a knife and fork, tore the toast and used it to spoon up the eggs. Maybe all five-year-old kids ate like that?

"Who did that to you?" Amy asked me, nodding at my face. I ignored her, because talking about it might well get me started on a path of recalling things that I wanted to forget. "Bet it was one of the Sheridan kids, yes?" she tutted and filled the coffee filter up. "Not that it would be Michelle, her being pregnant and soft as butter. Was it Scott? He's close to Daniel you know."

I ignored the questions, but I must have given something away, and in doing so I gave her enough ammunition to make an assumption.

"So, it was Daniel," she said, near-triumphant in her success. "He's come back from Charlotte and he's not the same. Terrible thing that happened to him there, terrible. But if he hit you, then you deserved it, so don't think you'll get sympathy here."

She'd been the first to turn her back on me nine years ago, and I wasn't going to let anything she said hurt me. I was done with letting her hurt me with her poisonous words.

Instead, I wanted to ask what had happened to Daniel in the city, but if I did that it would constitute talking to Amy and that wasn't happening.

Daniel had been out of control up at Isaac's grave, even I could see that.

Coffee made, I took a cup in to Rachel who was curled up on the sofa, surveying the overgrown yard. She thanked me, and tears rolled down her cheeks as if she couldn't stop them. I caught one and then cradled her face.

"Everything will be okay," I lied, again.

"What if Laurie has suffered some damage? I should have left."

"Could you have left?"

We hadn't talked about why she'd ended up with Callum, or the cult.

But we didn't need to when she glanced at me and shook her head. "No, not until… No, we couldn't."

"Until what? Why now? Why not before?"

She bowed her head. "Can we talk later?"

I wanted to talk about it then. I wanted to know why my beautiful sister had given over her life to a man who could do this to her. Wanted to know if he was Laurie's dad, and what had she been thinking having another baby with him. But, I couldn't push her, she was brittle and exhausted.

She pressed her hands to her belly. "What if there is no going back on what happened to Laurie?"

"He's young, Rachel. But maybe we need to get him to talk to someone, a specialist," I said, and then rethought the words as soon as they left my mouth. That was dangerous, letting him talk right now.

"I know. But what if the police find us because of that, what if they take me back and then I lose Laurie? What if they find out what I did?" The tears were back and I held her hand. "He needs help."

I didn't want to say out loud that she needed help as well.

"We'll figure it out," I said, and tried to sound like I meant it.

I had plans of how this would all work. They weren't fully formed, but whatever I did, she would be safe and with her babies. That was the way I could make things right in my world.

"Shhh," I said, and placed a finger on her lips. "I'll make it right, make it so you and Laurie can talk all you want about what happened to you. But, for now, we don't talk about what happened at the end."

"How will you make it right?"

I tugged her into a hug, "Trust your big brother." I knew it was a big ask, after everything in our lives, but I wanted to be there for her.

She sobbed more, curling in on herself. "Callum's gone, so why do I still feel so scared," she sounded broken.

I stroked her hair for a moment before stepping back. The urge to comfort her and make things right was strong. We'd always cared for each other all the way up until the point where we couldn't anymore, when she was in college and I'd spent time behind bars and then left Wyoming to find peace.

I would die for her though. That was blood. That was *right*.

It didn't help that all I could think about was the men in the shadows. Would they leave the compound? Would they come for Rachel and Laurie?

"I'll keep an eye on Laurie again," I said. That was the way I could help, by rounding up my five-year-old nephew and entertaining him.

When I went back to the kitchen, the toast and eggs were nearly gone and Aunt Amy was fussing around the boy. I'm not sure he entirely knew what to do with the cheek pinches and the hair tousling, and if anything, he was shrinking in on himself, immobile with fear.

"You done there?" I asked him and Amy rounded on me as I spoke.

"We need to talk," she said, determination in her voice. "It's not right you coming here."

I stopped her dead with a simple, "Not now,"

She subsided but kept giving me the *look*. The one I was used to, the one that spoke volumes about who I was and what my place was in this world. Loser. Failure. Murderer.

I helped Laurie get into his coat and pull on his boots. He needed more than what he had if he was going to live through a Wyoming winter. That meant a trip into town, or a drive out to Collier Springs where fewer people would stare and then punch me into gravestones. I'd already decided to go to Collier Springs for the cot I needed and some heaters, so I added clothes to the list. Anyway, going into Whisper Springs wasn't going to happen just yet. No way in hell I was going to let my past revisit my nephew until I was ready.

For the time being I could show him the horses and introduce him to the place that would one day be his. I needed to learn about him, show him some things, before everything caught up with us and I made it so it was me they took away.

We found Jeff in the barn. It didn't appear that he'd moved much from when I left him earlier in the day, and when he turned to see who was coming I saw he was favoring his left leg. So that was what this ranch had. A man in his sixties with a bum leg, and a woman who was trying to hold it all together. I'd sent them enough to hire some hands, where had the money gone? Were they even using it? They must have been to survive.

I explained more about the horses to Laurie. He seemed less scared and more interested this time. So, I talked the basics about respect and size and how much it hurt to get kicked or trodden on. I even showed him saddles and he was absorbed, excited even, disappointed when I said we weren't riding today but maybe in a few. He had a mini meltdown on the barn floor, but I let him get on with it, even though Jeff stared the entire time, bristling with disapproval.

What did he want me to do? The kid was stressed over something he couldn't have, he was vocalizing his disappointment, and hell, I wished I could've lain on the floor and kicked my legs and shouted in the hope I would get my way, or that things would be better.

"Kid needs his ass reddening," Jeff muttered, probably hoping I wouldn't hear him.

"I will put down the first person who touches Laurie."

"You're not welcome here, Micah," he snapped.

"I get that." I tried for calm, hauling back my instinct to start shouting.

"We have enough trouble as it is, without you coming back to mess it up. What you did won't ever be forgiven and your aunt lives with it every day."

I side-eyed him. "It's my ranch, Jeff. So back the f—hell off before I ask you to get off *my* property."

He wasn't going to be cowed. "Leave? Me and your aunt are the only things that are stopping your property from turning to shit."

I did a deliberate sweep on the run-down barn and recalled the mess I'd seen so far. "Seems to me that shit is a default setting here."

He bunched his fists. "I should finish what someone else started and take you down right here and now."

"You can try."

"We don't want you sending us your whoring drug money any more. It's wrong."

"Excuse me?"

"I don't know what laws you break to be able to send so much money, but you need to stop, it's killing your aunt to have to take it."

Wait. They thought the money I sent was the result of crime? Was this why the ranch was in such a bad state? Had they not been using it all? I opened my mouth to explain, and then shut it, because even though I fronted with defiance, I knew we were at an impasse. Without Jeff and Amy, the ranch would have been a distant memory, and without my money, wherever it came from, it would have failed a long time ago.

"I work for that money, and you'd better be investing it back in the ranch."

"We do okay," Jeff defended.

"Okay isn't paths that need clearing, or a damn water course that's changed direction after a rockfall."

"You're an asshole. Coming here thinking you can tell us what to do—"

"It's. My. Ranch."

"Micah?" Laurie interrupted my growing irritation. He was in front of me, his lower lip trembling, his tiny hands back into those fists. Last thing the kid needed was to witness a damn fight after everything else he'd seen. I scooped him up in my arms, and he hugged my neck, burying his face there.

"Not now," I said firmly to Jeff.

He subsided, and I knew this stupidity could go on forever or it could stop today. With plans for a family meeting firm in my head I left the barn, feeling as though maybe I could begin to pull the threads of my life together and make something permanent for my sister.

Until the cops came for us, at least.

I heard the sound of an engine, and the instant guilt and fear weighed heavily. With Laurie in my arms I went out to see who it was, spotting the car, and then the man who had climbed out of it.

Daniel. Standing in the front yard next to a shiny SUV, his arms folded over his chest, his stance firm, and every positive thought that had climbed out of my despair vanished.

"I came to apologize, Micah," he said. His tone was stiff; I didn't for one stinking minute think he felt sorry for what he'd done. I didn't need him to be repentant, I just needed him to leave me alone. It didn't matter he looked so good, the physical manifestation of so many of my fantasies, I wanted him to go.

"You need to get off my land," I said, and coughed at the catch in my voice. "You've had your say. I got the message."

He inspected his feet for a moment before looking up at me. Even though his body language was stiff his expression was remorseful. "I can't control my anger," he began.

I didn't want to hear excuses. "Please leave, Daniel."

"Sheriff says you're not pressing charges."

"Why would I do that?" I switched Laurie to my other side when he wriggled to be free, but I couldn't keep hold of him as he slithered down me and then hid behind my legs. There must have been something in the fear that Daniel saw, I don't know, I'm no expert, but kids are like scared kittens, or puppies, and most of us are wired to gentle ourselves around them.

"Hey," Daniel began and even at the short distance he crouched down. "I'm Daniel, what's your name?"

Laurie didn't move or respond. Why would he? He'd probably seen so much in his life, and this guy crouching in front of him was a stranger. Somehow though, he trusted me because his mom said he should. Kid was blind, obviously.

"I'm a doctor," Daniel added, but not even that helped. After a few seconds of the impasse he stood, brushing his hands on his pants. "You need to come to the clinic to get stitches," he added, and gestured at my face.

"I'll live."

"Micah, don't be stupid, I can help—"

I huffed a laugh, and pointed at my face. "You already helped enough."

"Please let me explain—"

"You need to go."

He was stricken. "I'm trying to say there are reasons." He rubbed his temples as if he was in pain, but none of that was enough for me to stand there and talk to him. "I want to make sure you know I didn't mean to hit you, that I was sorry—"

"Don't start with that sh—stuff. I let you get a hit in *this* time, but I won't let you again. We're done."

Daniel shook his head and grief filled his dark eyes. "You and me, Micah? It feels to me that we'll never be done."

"You're wrong, we were done the minute I took your keys nine years ago."

He paled, and closed his eyes briefly, and I imagined the wash of anger or despair that overcame him. He had every right to feel both things, but I didn't want that shit near Laurie right now.

He regarded me steadily and his expression softened, but I couldn't read it at all. I knew every inch of his face so well, but the man I recalled was twenty-two, not thirty-one, and he had some lines now.

Were they laughter lines? Or had he become forever sad?

When we used to kiss, he would laugh. Kisses had brought light into his eyes and I'd believed he wanted me.

After a softly spoken goodbye to Laurie, and with no visible signs of anger, he climbed back into his brand-new SUV. Seems like *Doctor* Daniel Sheridan made bank, and that was my last thought before going into the house.

Only when I sat quietly in the bunkhouse, wrapped in blankets and falling asleep did I think back on his final words. *We'll never be done.*

I'd loved him as much as a nineteen-year-old could, and in one stupid move, one moment of self-doubt and childish insanity, I'd destroyed it all. But whatever his anger was, he had no right to punish me after all that time. Right?

I was cold. Alone. And now, I couldn't sleep.

Fuck. My. Life.

I pulled out my cell and checked the news one more time. *Just in case.* And then I typed various search terms and finally, after some clicking around, I found Doctor Daniel Sheridan's name, and the connection to a hospital in Charlotte, NC, and then to research what he was involved in, and then to a news link.

A shooting.

The details were formulaic, the kind of thing I would see, far too often, in the news. A lone gunman had held doctors, nurses, and administrators hostage. There had been a death, a female doctor, mom to a new baby, and then details of how the gunman had taken his own life right after shooting her. The photos were of police tape around the ER, and groups of, what I assumed, were cops and SWAT guys dealing with the situation.

And right in the group of huddled survivors, his eyes wide and his face white, was Daniel.

Survivor.

8

DANIEL

I PULLED THE CAR TO THE SIDE OF THE ROAD AS SOON AS I left Lennox land and shut off the engine. What the hell had I just done? Neil had said he'd handle it, that he'd come back and tell me the full extent of the trouble I was in. But when he came in and told me that Micah wanted nothing to do with me, that he wasn't pressing charges, I didn't feel relief.

I needed to pay now. It was my turn for him to pummel me into the ground. Maybe if he did that I could restart my fucking life.

Something needed to restart it.

Nausea gripped me, a familiar feeling these days. I rested my head on the steering wheel, closing my eyes and running through all the exercises I'd learned to control the chaos in my head. The flashbacks had stopped, the nightmares had eased, but I was far from over what had happened to me. Add in Micah coming home, and that was it, I was done.

My knuckles hurt—but his face—I'd split his lip.

I couldn't breathe and flung open the door. The frigid air, threatening more snow, bit sharply into my face. I stepped into the cold darkness, tugging my coat close, grabbing my flashlight and slamming the car door. Then I walked, away from my car, up the small hill by the road and along the brow of it. I didn't have a direction in mind but wasn't surprised when I ended up at the stone bridge that crossed the Whisper Ridge Creek. There used to be the remains of a wooden bridge, but after the accident that had destroyed so many lives nine years ago, the town had erected this stone bridge, wide enough to walk over, and no more. There was a small plaque on the side, but I didn't need to read it to know what it said. It held a single name Isaac, and a date, December 2009, and three letters. RIP. I traced the name in the wet snow, then fished out my gloves as the wind chill seeped into my coat.

No one could stand for long in the bitter wind, and the warmth of the car was a blessing.

I knew I had to go and see Chris and tell him that Micah was back. I was just delaying the inevitable. He would be back soon. I parked up outside his place and waited, tipping my head back and closing my eyes. I must have fallen asleep, or at least rested at that point where I wasn't entirely conscious.

The bang on the window sent me upright and smacking my head on the ceiling, cursing, and grabbing at my chest in shock.

Chris peered through the window at me, and he looked contrite, but then grinned, when he saw me reeling backward. I opened the door on him in retribution and really the only person that hurt was me when my door smacked his wheelchair.

"What are you doing in the chair?" I asked as I straightened up.

"Long day," Chris said with a smile. I remembered a time when he'd hated using it, but he was cool about the need for it now. Or at least that was the impression he gave anyone who asked, but I hadn't been home in a while so I might have missed big chunks about how he was getting on.

He expertly wheeled himself up the small ramp and into his house, and I followed, closing the door behind me and then not moving from that spot.

"What?" Chris stared up at me.

I cut straight to the chase. "Micah Lennox is back."

Chris levered himself up and out the chair, stretching tall, and then strode into his kitchen. In jeans, as he was, you couldn't tell he had a prosthetic leg from the left knee down. He walked so confidently, and with his back to me and his scars hidden from view, it appeared as if nothing had touched his life. He kept fit, worked at the local high school as a sports coach and taught English, but I wished he had been what he was meant to be, and my heart still ached with the loss of his dreams.

He began to make coffee and I leaned against the door jamb. "Didn't you hear me? Micah is back in town."

Chris placed two mugs side by side on the counter, and the only evidence he had heard and was processing the words was that he was quiet. That and the fact he traced the scars on his face with his fingers. Something he did when he was thinking hard.

"I know," he finally said after a short while. "Miriam told Nancy, whose daughter is friends with Liam in my class. The text came in at eleven-fifteen, within five minutes the entire bus knew, and of course, so did I." He explained everything so carefully, as if it was vital I understood the process.

"Chris, I'm sorry."

He rounded on me. "What are *you* sorry for?"

That Micah took my keys, drove my car, that I didn't think I had to stop him.

"That you had to find out that way," I said instead.

He shrugged and went back to concentrating on coffee. His shoulders were stiff and he leaned forward so his hip rested on the counter. Then he braced his hands there and sighed.

"Everyone knows what happened back then," he began. "But when the kids started with the Chinese whispers, I stopped them. By the time it had reached the ones sitting behind me, I was some kind of ghost, a kid who'd died and been resurrected from the dead." He smiled at me and shrugged, "I'd prefer it if they stuck to my past being that of a badass ninja, but hey I can't control gossip. You know what it's like, these kids have seen me like this since they were little, and everyone knows what really happened, but I got the coach to pull over and gathered them around me and I told the kids everything in no uncertain terms. I told them that the three of us were young, we were idiots, we shouldn't have been in the car, it was a bad accident, and that they needed to remember, when they finally drove, to be responsible drivers." He snorted. "Hell, it turned out to be a teachable experience."

Chris and I hadn't talked about the accident since I'd found him trying to kill himself when the horror of what had happened to him had become too much to handle. I couldn't face up to it until now, but I wasn't in a better place at that moment to be able to talk rationally. He sounded as if he could handle the memories of it all.

"How can you be so blasé about this?" I asked. I couldn't believe he was leaning there as if none of this mattered, talking about his day as if he hadn't had to explain his life story to a bus full of kids.

I STOPPED by my parent's place after the store. Chris had called me, asked me to fetch salad, which was the weirdest thing ever. Chris didn't like salad, never had. I like to think that this was an excuse to see me before I went back to Charlotte on the weekend.

"Chris?"

The kitchen was empty, Dad at work, Mom volunteering as she always did on a Tuesday, had only recently gone back. It had been a hard year for her, caring for Chris, but it had been Chris who had told her to go back.

"Chris?" I called again. I expected he'd be in the front room, using the stairs to get to his room was hell on him at the moment, but when I didn't see him, it was okay. I was proud of my little brother for managing the stairs and getting himself up to his bedroom.

"I got you lettuce, like three different types," I called up to him, and spent a few minutes trying to fit it all in my parent's fridge. When I shut the door I saw the letter, and I hated it was pinned right there. An offer to Chris for a pro-ball tryout. It had arrived when he was in the hospital, and I don't know why he insisted on keeping it on the fridge. Surely it was a reminder of what he'd lost.

Still, not one of us took it down. This was his decision.

I made coffee, hunted down the latest batch of cookies, and took the whole lot, precariously balanced, up the stairs, stopping to rearrange it all half way up. I put it on the table inside Chris' room, a hospital table on wheels that slid up to his bed. He didn't use it anymore but no one had taken it back to the hospital. Never mind, it was kind of useful.

The bathroom door was ajar, "Chris, coffee, and I found macadamia and choc chip, stole loads of them for us."

There was silence from the bathroom.

"Chris?"

I didn't want to just walk in. My brother had lost a lot of self-respect this past year, people poking at him all the time, and I was desperate to preserve what little dignity he had right now.

But.

It was so quiet.

I knocked on the door, called his name, and pushed on the door to widen the space.

My brother was on the floor, curled into a fetal position, the empty bottle of pills next to him, and scrawled on the mirror with a Sharpie:

"No more, sorry."

CHRIS HUFFED A LAUGH. "What do you want me to do Daniel? You were there at the beginning, after the accident, there when I woke up. You found me when I tried to kill myself, but then you left to go back to college. You missed the parts of my life where I railed at anyone I could about the injustice of what happened. The bits where guilt and hate nearly finished off what the accident had started. Then you also missed the realization that I had one life, and a family who loved me, and I wanted it to be a good life. I'm done with the hate, and if I see Micah, I'll probably end up shaking his hand, and asking him how he's been."

"You mean what he's done after his time in prison," I couldn't help the bitterness in my voice. Chris stared at me and there was a disappointment even I could read.

"A year in prison is enough for any man who was paying for something he shouldn't have."

"He took my car, he drove it, he killed Isaac, hurt you."

I genuinely have no idea how Chris could be so centered about this. He'd had everything laid out in front of him, a pro-ball career, a wife, kids, a future. And what did he have now? A teaching position at a school no more than half a mile from where he was born.

Chris was the one of the Sheridan kids who was supposed to see the world.

And look how that turned out.

We'd never had a real talk about how he felt though, and I knew part of him must've blamed me for my part in that fateful night. He had every right to. Chris finished the coffee and handed me a cup, then led me out of the kitchen and into his front room where I sank into the sofa with the view out over his yard. It amazed me just how beautiful Chris's yard was, even in winter it was a palette of greens against the snow.

Was I amazed because he was the only one in our family who had a green thumb? Or was it that he had managed to create such beauty even being an amputee. I wish I knew how to separate pride in my brother, and regret about what happened.

Chris settled into his own chair and then inhaled the fragrance of the coffee. He was tired, but well, and seeing him like that was a tick in the column for staying in Whisper Ridge permanently. I'd spent far too long away from my family with college, and medical school, then a residency and ER medicine. I wanted to see Michelle's baby, watch Chris live his life, if I could get past the hurdle of confronting the past with him. I needed to see Scott talk himself into land deals. I wanted to be here when Mark graduated and be at the big family party. Hell, I wanted pot roast at Mom and Dad's on a Sunday, and to be doctor to a new generation of Whisper Ridge patients.

At least I think I did.

Finally, Chris began to talk. "I love my life, you know. The teaching, working with the kids on the all-ability teams, being an advocate for all-ability sports. Who knows if I'd ever have made it to pro-ball anyway?"

"You would have," I was fiercely proud of what any of my siblings could do.

He shrugged. "Just accept that I *am* happy, okay?"

Was this it? The great discussion I'd been fearing? Was it possible that Chris's even-tempered outlook on his new life, one where he was happy, was enough to make the worry lessen?

"Okay."

"Have you seen Micah?" Chris asked.

"At Isaac's grave, I hit him." Instinctively I hid my knuckles but in doing that I drew his attention to them and Chris's smile dropped.

"What the fuck, Daniel?"

I put my coffee down and stood. I wanted to explain about the anger inside me, the guilt, the memories of the accident that merged so inextricably with the memories of what happened to me in the city. But then, I didn't want to talk about any of it at all.

Least of all to Chris. We were good brothers, as long as we kept all the mess hidden and to one side. That was the way it worked for me.

I shook my head as he began to stand.

"Don't get up, I need to go, but I just wanted you to know he was here, and if you need me…"

"If I did need you what would you do? Run the other way?" He was so damned disappointed. "Daniel, please don't go, I thought you wanted to talk, let's talk, we haven't done that in a long time."

"Another time, I'll see you at Sunday dinner," I said and left as fast as I could. The walls were closing in and I needed to get outside.

9

DANIEL

I KNEW I'D GET CALLS AS SOON AS I WAS HOME, BECAUSE Chris would have contacted at least one of the family with concerns over the way I'd left and what I had done to Micah. Dad was first, wanting to ask me if I knew which button to press to get his address book up on his laptop. It was a ploy, so as to ask me how I was. As a doctor he would understand PTSD, and I could've probably told him about the lack of sleep and the dreams that visited me and twisted the past and the present together.

Instead, I explained how I was absolutely fine and that he should get Michelle to look at his laptop because I was crap with technology.

Mom's excuse was to check I was still going for dinner on Sunday.

"I told you I was yesterday."

"Good," she offered, and then I knew what was coming next. "How are you, sweetheart?"

"I'm good. Anyway, I have to go, I have notes to work on. Bye. Love you."

I didn't even give her the chance to say anything else, ending the call as soon as *love you* left my mouth.

Scott didn't even bother hiding why he was calling.

"Heard you punched Micah," he said. "I don't know whether to be proud or pissed," Scott summed up his feelings, cursed, and then ended the call and didn't ask me how I was.

I didn't even answer Michelle's call, then felt guilty because, hey, pregnant lady, and phoned her back. I just said I was fine and that I didn't want to talk about it.

She listened to my words and said a simple, *oh, Daniel.* It broke me to hear her tone.

When Mark called from college I thought that the entire thing was getting way out of hand. He wanted to know how my counseling was going, and that even though he understood why I might have hit Micah, did I nearly have to kill him?

God, talk about exaggeration.

"I didn't nearly kill him. I punched him once, then he shoved me away."

"Scott said it was *really* bad, like blood everywhere."

I never felt all of my thirty-one years as much as I did talking to my twenty-one-year-old youngest brother.

"Scott is talking out of his ass," I summarized, "I'm good. Micah's fine," I ended the call with a promise to visit him in Chicago.

Why wasn't I allowed to have complicated issues that I needed to deal with by myself? What was it about my family that they felt they had to be all up in my business?

They care about you.

They were what you thought about when you had a gun

at your temple. So, stop fucking about and tell them what happened in the city, and how you are trying to deal with it, and why you're such a fucking miserable bastard.

And why seeing Micah made you crave all those things you thought you once had, like love, and sex, and affection.

When my cell vibrated with yet another call I almost threw the thing across the room, but the number was one I couldn't ignore. The practice emergency line.

"Doctor Sheridan speaking, can I help?"

"Doctor, this is Amy Reynolds at the Lennox Ranch, could you spare us a visit?"

My heart skipped at the name Lennox, as if someone had poked at me with a sharp stick.

"What's the nature of the visit?"

Halfheartedly, I imagined Micah keeling over in a ditch, which would've solved all my problems.

There was a pause, Amy evidently considering the situation, and I had just reached the edge of annoyed at the empty silence when she sighed.

"Between you and me doctor, my niece is here, Rachel, and she'd kill me if she knew I was calling you, and I didn't really want to, but she's expecting, and looks ill."

Amy stopped, and I waited for more. When she remained quiet, I filled in the blanks. "And you'd like me to visit."

"If it's not too much bother."

I was already gathering my gear. "How many weeks pregnant is she?" I needed to assess if I should get the team midwife from the hospital there.

"I'm not sure, but she refuses to leave the house, and her son is crying so hard. Can you come out?"

I checked the time. "Can you give me any idea what's wrong?" I was already up and shrugging on my coat, then picked up my bag and checked for my keys.

"I honestly don't know what to say," Amy sounded bewildered.

That could mean anything. "Is she in labor?"

"No, at least I don't think so."

Whisper Ridge wasn't big enough for an ambulance or a paramedic, I was all they had with backup from Collier Springs and that was a two-ward hospital, to the east of us. "I'll be there in twenty." I would go, assess, get her to the hospital if needed. It was all about decisions, and I could make those in my sleep. I connected with Patsy, the midwife on rotation to cover emergencies.

"Doctor Sheridan?" she sounded out of breath.

"Where are you right now?" I asked.

"The hospital, Emma's in labor. Is there an emergency?"

Not anything bigger than Emma Warren in labor, she was forty-three, pregnant with triplets after treatment and it would be all hands-on deck. Anyway, I hadn't even assessed Rachel Lennox, and I kicked myself that I was reacting like this just to have back up to go to the Lennox Ranch.

"Nothing I can't handle, I'll send you notes. Good luck with the triplets."

The plow was out and I had to wait at the end of my drive for it. I exchanged waves with the driver before following it out of town and up the rise to Lennox land.

I tried not to think about my earlier visit, the humiliation of having lost control, the pain of what I'd done evident in my hand and on Micah's face. I was ashamed and not entirely sure what to do with the power of that embarrassment except turn it back on myself.

By the time I reached the ranch house I had shut down anything but the part of me that was being a doctor.

Amy was at the door, there was no sign of Micah, and she ushered me straight into a back room and to a woman I barely recognized. I'd last seen Rachel Lennox a long time before the Christmas of the accident. She'd left as soon as she could for college, disappeared as if she'd never existed in this town at all, but I recall when she left she'd had some life in her, hope for the future, despite the parents she was running from.

This woman lying there, on her side, was thin, marked by exhaustion and beaten down, and it wasn't just the pregnancy, which was advanced. There was bruising on her face, and neck and when I examined the patterns they seemed to be finger shaped. Compassion rushed through me as I imagined someone hurting her.

"Hey Rachel, you remember me?"

She glanced up at me, and her eyes were bloodshot. "Daniel Sheridan. Scott's brother."

I would always be Scott's brother to her. She'd been in his year at school and I often thought my little brother had been sweet on her. I crouched next to her and held her hand. "That's right; Amy was telling me you're not feeling so well."

She tried to tug her hand away. "I'm fine."

Thing is, she couldn't bullshit a bullshitter. I'd spent so long telling people I was fine that I could see right through her.

"I'm a doctor," I explained. "So, it's okay to talk to me about your baby."

She rolled onto her back, wincing. "I don't need anything."

"Why don't you answer my questions and I'll be the judge of that?"

"Micah won't like it," she said, and sent a worried glance toward the hallway, as if he was standing there. I released her hand and shut the door, and then went back to her.

"Then we won't tell him."

She appeared to consider that and then nodded sharply. I don't think it was agreement after weighing up the offer, I think it was resignation that I was crouched there staring at her.

"Okay, let's start with some simple stuff. Your date of birth."

I scribbled down everything she told me, her name she gave as Rachel Lennox. This was her sixth pregnancy, the third had been a complete birth with no complications and at home. She'd lost four babies through miscarriage—all past the twelve-week mark. When I pressed her for details, she just clutched her belly and stayed quiet, so I backed off. If it had been a medical reason, then she would have told me, right? Which led me to think that something about the way she lived, her environment, drugs maybe, or possibly the person who'd laid their hands on her, had caused the miscarriages. She was also thirty-something weeks pregnant, at least she thought she was, but she told me she'd lost track of time.

"That happens," I said. "First thing my patients tell me

is that being pregnant makes you forgetful. I'm not pregnant, yet I need a diary to remind me of everything."

I realized I'd slipped quite easily into using my patented bedside manner and at least she gave me a small smile.

I did all the usual checks, listened to the baby's heartbeat and let her listen. The baby was moving well, although I agreed it was okay when she said the movements were less than they had been because there wasn't as much room. I made a note of Rachel's blood pressure, asked her to do a urine test so I could check, then took some measurements.

"I put you around the time you think you are," I explained. I wasn't a midwife, so I didn't have the unerring instinct of someone who brought babies into the world all the time, but I knew my job. "Thirty-two to thirty-four weeks. How are you feeling? And don't say fine."

She began to cry then, huge tears that collected in her eyes and slid down her face. Her tears reminded me of the way Michelle could cry at the drop of a hat due to pregnancy hormones, but this was more than that. Was it just exhaustion and emotional overload, or more? I held her hand, seeing the naked emotion and knowing this was bigger than being pregnant.

"I'm here to talk if you need me," I said. "Doctor-patient confidentiality is a thing you know."

She shook her head slowly. "I can't," she said, and there was a hint of fear in her tone. "We said, Micah said…no, it's okay."

Was she scared of Micah? Had Micah put the bruises

on her temple and left arm? No, whatever had happened in our past, he'd been gentle with his sister and I had to believe for Rachel's sake that he was gentle still.

There was a knock on the door, and Micah's voice. "Everything okay?"

"We're okay," she called, and then squeezed my hand. "I'm good," she lied to my face.

"I'd like you to come down to the clinic to see the midwife," I put a comment on her notes, "in the next few days."

"Yes, doctor." She said the words but I'm not sure she actually meant them, as she wouldn't meet my eyes.

"Are you registered with a hospital? Seeing a midwife? Taking vitamins?"

She still refused to meet my eye, and some instinct told me I shouldn't press for answers.

I left her then, after an encouraging pat to her arm, and found Micah leaning on the wall outside the room. He straightened immediately and was concerned.

I started to speak before he had a chance to ask me a thing. "Who put those bruises on her?" I stepped close to him but he didn't back down.

"Is everything okay?" he said instead of answering my question. But I'd seen a lot in my time in the ER and that wasn't the question of a guilty man, but of someone desperately worried about a patient I was dealing with. So, if he hadn't hurt her, then why was he telling her not to talk to anyone, and why the hell was she so scared of Micah not being happy she talked?

"Daniel, please, is she okay?"

I could have given Micah the speech about how she

was his sister not his wife, and that I didn't share information, but I couldn't face another moment of him pleading with me.

I'd beaten the man, giving him the split lip—that was on *me.* Guilt alone was enough to make me feel as if I needed to do something to take the worry from me.

Christ, this man ties me in knots.

I gave the standard reply. "Mother and baby are doing okay."

I went to move past him but he stopped me with a soft touch to the arm. When I looked at him I saw right into his light gray eyes, framed by familiar long lashes. He'd always had the most beautiful eyes. He used to complain that I was a freak when I told him that. I'd just ignored him back then.

"You're not lying to me?"

I didn't know what to say to that. I mean, of course I wasn't lying, I wouldn't. But, did he think that because I was so angry with him, after I'd left him at Isaac's grave, that I would take out that anger on Rachel?

Of course, he thinks that. Why would he think anything else?

"I don't lie," I snapped.

He huffed a laugh, "We both know that isn't true."

I held his accusing stare.

"Make sure you get her to the clinic call ahead to check the midwife is there, failing that get her to see someone over in Collier Springs, and get her vitamins. Look after her, for God's sake."

All he did was nod and that made me mad, and anxious, and a hundred other conflicting emotions. Then he followed me out to my car, shrugging on his thick coat, his Stetson low on his head.

"You seeing me off the property?" I quipped because the silence was awkward.

"Thank you for seeing her, you didn't have to."

I rounded on him. "I'm a doctor, what else did you think I'd do?" He winced, and I knew immediately and exactly what he'd thought. "You imagined I'd hear it was her, connect it to you, and not bother?"

"I wouldn't blame you."

And there it was, lying between us. Him thinking the worst of me and me not being able to explain how I was feeling.

But, whatever, I was a doctor and I did my job well.

I left quickly without saying anything else and drove all the way to the edge of the ranch again, before stopping. The implication I would let what happened nine years ago affect my ability as a doctor, stung. Also, that barb about lying had hit home, and a confused mess of guilt and shame filled me. I knew he was talking about the accident. I slammed my hands on the steering wheel. That hadn't been my lie, that had been about protecting my family, and punishing the man who had put Chris in a coma.

Micah had insisted I'd said he could borrow my car anytime. I had denied it and told the cops he'd stolen it. I knew that was a lie, and maybe I was wrong to tell them that, but pain and anger had made me say it. I'd wanted him to suffer. I'd said he could borrow the car, but not specifically that evening, and it was that which meant I could justify my actions. He would have got time either way, my white lie had meant nothing to the prosecution, or so they said. Whether I'd given my permission or not, he'd still driven the car recklessly, and that was his crime.

Lie or not he'd needed to do time for what he'd done to my brother and Isaac. It didn't matter how he got behind bars. Back then, I'd just wanted him to pay.

The remorse was just another part of the tangled mess in my head.

10

MICAH

I LET RACHEL SLEEP THE NEXT MORNING, PENNING A NOTE for when she woke up. I occupied Laurie as best I could with talking about horses, and then bundled him into the truck and headed for Collier Springs and the biggest, but most local strip mall, I could find. Laurie stood for a long time just inside the entrance to a large factory outlet store surrounded by a few smaller shops. His eyes were wide and he was clearly panicking. This was more than just a stubborn refusal to move, and then he began to hyperventilate, I scooped him up and reassured him that nothing in a mall would hurt him.

At first, he wriggled, and then he went silent, and somehow, after a few hurried gasps he began to relax as if he trusted me. He gripped my neck, which made shopping a little difficult. It was only when we looked for clothes for him that he actually loosened his hold and sat comfortably in my arms. I considered putting him in the seat on the cart, but that might have made him feel as if he was trapped, and he weighed nothing so he was easy to hold.

He had no opinion on clothes, but the stuff he was wearing, jeans too short for him, a T-shirt that swamped his body and a sweatshirt with the sleeves cut, wasn't exactly much to have to live up to.

I'd left the ranch I worked at in a rush, with no belongings other than my phone and a charger. So, I bought myself jeans, shirts, sweaters, and then did the same thing for Rachel and Laurie, coats, gloves, scarves, and we were set for whatever the Wyoming winter could throw at us. I found a cot which would be enough for the short time I would be there, a couple of oil filled heaters, and I even picked up baby things, including newborn diapers, just in case. Who the hell knew what Rachel needed? But, I pulled up a list on Google anyway, and bought one of everything, because if she had gone into labor yesterday we had nothing. I also read the comments to the post, something about extra pacifiers, and diapers, so I did that, and the cart was near to full.

Vitamins, as Daniel had instructed, were a little more problematic. What did a pregnant woman need? I checked Google again, and this time I read deeper, got frustrated at the amount of information, and picked up every vitamin on the shelf. Maybe Rachel would know better? Or I could ask the midwife when we saw her.

Not that Rachel wanted to see a midwife. That had been the one thing she'd kept saying before we left.

"I gave birth to Laurie on my own, I can do it again."

It broke my heart she'd been alone. It killed me that I hadn't even known I'd had a nephew, and I hugged him briefly. He made a noise of discouragement, but clung to me, so I think he was mostly okay with his emotional uncle testing the limits of hugs.

I wandered the toy aisle waiting for Laurie to tell me to stop to have a closer look at something he was interested in. Action Man? Was that a decent choice? They all seemed to come with tiny guns, and I didn't think that was a good thing. I picked up a kid's board game, Chutes and Ladders, and some brightly colored books, and poked it all as best I could in the cart. After that I was lost.

I mean what did *normal* five-year olds want? At least, the ones who hadn't spent the start of their life locked away from the world? The kids I'd taught at my old job were all older, in their teens, and they were all about mobile phones and handheld games, but given where Laurie had spent his first five years, I doubted that was something he wanted. Or needed.

He seemed as lost as I was, and then his gaze focused on the jigsaw display. He actually squirmed down to examine them, held my hand and tugged me closer, apparently enamored with the myriad of designs. Maybe Rachel had access to jigsaws at the compound? Who knew, but this was what he wanted, and he chose of varying difficulties, some that I thought would be way too challenging for his age. Still, I didn't argue and they joined the clothes in the shopping cart.

"Mom helps me," he explained as we waited at the checkout, holding my hand tight. "Will you help me too, sir?"

That was the longest sentence I'd heard from him.

"Of course, I will, and you can call me Uncle Micah if you like." He nodded as if I'd given him a precious gift, and then wrinkled his nose. He seemed to be thinking hard about something, contemplating consequences; there was an old soul in his pale eyes.

"I got one with horses for you," he said after that pause, and waited for an answer.

"I love jigsaws with horses on them."

I'd never actually done a jigsaw that I could remember, but I'd clearly said the right thing.

I ruffled his blond hair and he smiled up at me. Not a grin, not the smile of a kid who had a whole load of toys, but a smile that filled his eyes with light. I couldn't help but smile back.

"Well, hell, Micah Lennox, is that you?"

I stiffened at the question. Jesus, how far from Whisper Ridge did I have to go to avoid someone who would want to talk to me? I turned to face the owner of the voice, and the bottom fell out of my carefully calm shopping trip.

Fuck my life. Daniel's sister, Michelle. Another connection to Chris, and everything I'd done. Not someone else I have to look in the eyes and stay my ground.

"Michelle," I said, and glanced at her belly. She was way bigger than Rachel, near ready to give birth. She seemed healthier than Rachel, in a dress made for pregnancy, her hair styled, and a huge diamond on her left hand. This was what I wanted for Rachel and regret swamped me that she wouldn't have this. I'd picked up some loose skirts and shirts in the maternity aisle, but I was a ranch hand who lived in jeans and sweatshirts. What did I know about pregnant women and what they wore?

Ask Michelle.

Don't talk to Michelle.

"Two weeks to go," she answered my unspoken question, and rubbed her belly, then smiled at me. Smiling disarmed me. She should've carried the same anger as Daniel, so why wasn't she trying to hit me, or demand I leave. “How are you?” she asked instead, and waited expectantly.

“I’m good,” I lied. I was in the middle of a shopping mall, buying clothes, with my overwhelmed, emotionally scarred, nephew, hoping for anonymity and ending up talking to the sister of the guy who’d hit me and hated me. How was today even real?

“Aww, Micah, I’m so sorry, Daniel hurt you good,” she said, and reached up to touch my face. I backed away and knocked into the cart. “My bad,” she said, immediately resting her hand back on her belly.

She’d tried to touch me, I’d overreacted. She was embarrassed. I was ashamed. And now, we’d run out of polite conversation. What else could we talk about? The last time we’d met she’d seen me in the hospital and had tried to hug me, wanted to fucking *forgive* me. I hadn’t wanted her hugs then, nor her forgiveness, and I didn’t need either of them.

Not when I’d hurt her brother and killed another.

Right now, she’d asked me if I was okay, told me she was having a baby, we’d covered the fact that her brother had taken his moment to hit me, and I was kind of done. Only we were trapped in this line. This was my idea of hell. Laurie tugged at my jeans and I scooped him up into my arms.

“Oh, who is this little cutie?” Michelle asked.

Laurie buried his face in my neck.

“He’s not good with strangers,” I explained, although why I bothered, I didn’t know. I just wanted to get out of there without connecting to another person, let alone a Sheridan. What I’d just said left me open to a discussion about kids and their fears.

"Oh sweetheart, I know what you mean," Michelle said to Laurie, not me. "I hate coming to these places, all this noise and color. What do you think of having a sister or brother? Doctor Daniel tells me your momma is having a baby just like me." Laurie still didn't glance up, but he relaxed a little. "Hey, what about my baby being friends with your baby, what would you think of that?"

I opened my mouth to answer but Laurie beat me to it.

"No friends," he snapped.

"Okay. That's okay." She looked at me briefly, and there were so many questions written on her expression. Luckily, I didn't have to answer any of them because Laurie spoke loudly.

"I'll look after *my* baby," he said, fiercely.

Michelle was startled but tempered it with a smile. "It's a huge job being a *big* brother. You'll be fabulous at it."

"No one will hurt it," Laurie added, and then buried his face again.

I willed it to be our turn at the checkout when Michelle's eyes brightened with emotion.

"Micah?" she said softly. In that single word were those questions; had Laurie been hurt, what did he mean, why was he so quietly determined that he would protect his new sibling?

Thankfully the line moved and it was our turn and I could offer Michelle my back, packing things randomly in bags, all one-handed, paying and then near running with the cart to my truck.

How fucking stupid was this, that I was trying to outrun a pregnant woman so I didn't have to talk to her?

We made it back to the ranch just as it grew dark, unpacked clothes and baby supplies into Rachel's room, and the rest to the bunkhouse for me. It would do for a little while. Only when I was sure Laurie was settled with his mom did I leave the house and call Henry Boville Junior, the owner of the spread an hour outside Denver that I'd walked away from to go to Rachel.

He answered on the third ring.

"Micah, hey. Hell, when you coming back, the students miss you, and Jem is pining."

That hit hard. I missed Jem, he was my horse, a gorgeous quarter horse. And the kids, I missed them too.

Or at least, I missed them when Henry mentioned them, but to be honest I'd not given them much of a thought up until then.

"Henry, I need a bit more time."

Henry laughed. He was a good guy, about my age. He held the financial reins of the Split-K ranch, about an hour outside Denver. I'd landed on my feet working for him. He didn't care about the record I had, and I'd been there for seven years now. There was very little I didn't know about the running of the Split-K, and I was more Henry's right hand than ranch hand. I worked with the horse training, I earned big bonuses, made a name for myself.

I wish I'd been able to work my own place, spend my life on the Lennox Ranch, but that was never going to happen.

"No worries, bud, it's quiet here, and I have Arnie working with the students who can still get here through the snow."

The K was as remote as the Lennox Ranch, and so they got cut off in the worst of the storms. They wouldn't be busy in winter, given they were a horse breeding operation, with no land allocated to cattle.

"Poor kids," I joked. Arnie wasn't the most patient with the teenagers and what he called their phone obsession.

"Is everything okay with you? Anything I can do to help?"

He'd been there with me when Rachel had called, begging me for help. Hell, he'd helped me take the tarpaulins off my truck and get the thing started.

"Nah, it's all good. I just need a couple weeks."

"As long as you're back for spring…"

Henry Junior was joking, but under it there was a thread of pleading and the need for reassurance. How in god's name could I reassure him when I didn't know what was going to happen.

As when the cops were called to the scene of a murder back where I'd helped Rachel. Or when someone pointed a finger at my sister, and then at me?

"Of course."

We ended the call with the usual bro type stuff, I counted Henry as a close friend, maybe my only friend. I travelled light in life, and it was the only way I knew how to be now. I missed the K, wished for a split-second that I was back there with my uncomplicated life and limited responsibilities.

But I'd made a choice, which was not a choice at all. Rachel, Laurie, and the unborn baby, had to be my priority.

Now I had to find a way to live with it.

11

MICAH

RACHEL WAS PLEASED WITH THE THINGS I'D BOUGHT Laurie. She spent a long time checking them out, and pairing things up. I'd even got the sizes right apparently, although the coat meant for a five-year-old swamped his tiny body. Still, you could never have enough extra coat space in a Wyoming winter.

The things I'd bought her she didn't comment on, piling them onto the cabinet in her room, neatly and precisely. She thanked me though, and for the vitamins. The tiny sleepsuits I'd bought for the baby, along with diapers, and pacifiers, were placed carefully in drawers, and I think I even saw a small smile at one point. Laurie helped her sort the baby stuff out, and took a serious amount of focused time making sure all the items were placed in some kind of order that made him happy.

I waited until Jeff and Amy were both in the house and Rachel was with Laurie. She'd commandeered the kitchen table to do one of the easier jigsaws with Laurie and I gestured for Jeff and Amy to step into the front room.

"We need to talk," I announced, and waited for them to come up with a million reasons why they weren't happy to sit down and discuss matters.

Instead, Jeff and Amy exchanged glances and then moved into the front room and took seats next to each other on the long sofa.

I sat opposite and judged their expressions. Amy looked as if she was going to cry, Jeff wouldn't meet my gaze and his cheeks were flushed. I assumed he was angry, but I wasn't sure what would make Amy want to cry.

Then in one short sharp sentence she made everything clear.

"This is our only home, you can't make us leave," she blurted out, and blindly sought her husband's hand, which Jeff took without argument.

I blinked at them both. "I'm not asking you to leave," I said.

"We know this is your land, your house," Jeff blurted, "know we're just caretakers, but we're not getting any younger and we'll fight you for the rights to stay here. We spoke to a lawyer, and he said you can't get rid of us, not after everything we've done."

His chest rose and fell rapidly with anger and frustration.

"Without us, you wouldn't have a room to sit in," Amy snapped, and I could see she was getting angry.

"Hold on," I held up a hand. "Wait a minute. No one is throwing anyone out. Hell, we owe you everything that you stayed here when Rachel and I couldn't. But, this is my land, and I want Rachel to make a home here. She'll need her own place that she can bring the kids up on, and she'll need her Aunt Amy and Uncle Jeff, okay. So, no one is leaving."

I sat back in the chair and waited for their reaction. I was going to fight this corner. Amy and Jeff were Rachel's only family and she needed the Lennox Ranch to make a life for herself.

Amy regarded me with concentration, and then leaned forward in her seat, still gripping Jeff's arm.

"But you're not staying," she said, picking up on the absence of information about my plans. I had so many answers I could've given. That I couldn't stay because I had promised nine years ago to never come back. Or that if the authorities caught up with us then I'd already decided what I was going to do. Or maybe, that I had a job on a ranch elsewhere. I decided to avoid details.

"No."

Jeff looked relieved, and I think Amy seemed disappointed. I didn't know how to fight both battles, so I ignored them and forged ahead.

"I want to hire in some guys and get the land taken care of," Jeff opened his mouth to defend himself but I didn't need to hear it. "Jeff, you're one man and this land is a bitch. I want the creek back, the landfall fenced, I want the bunkhouse fixed, plans put in place for a couple of hands up to here to help you. We don't have the cash to deal with this so I will be talking to Scott about the offer on the land to the east."

"You want to sell some of the ranch?" Amy was horrified. "Let them build condos and God knows what on your Papa's land?"

"Mine. It's all mine at the moment. Selling off part of it means we can get Rachel a place built, secure her future, invest in this place, keep it for Laurie and his brother or sister. Then when I'm gone I'll be deeding the whole lot to Rachel for her and the kids."

Jeff seemed about ready to meet my gaze so I let him talk.

"It's all we can do, we're land rich and cash poor, and young Scott assures me this will be luxury housing, seasonal owners buying into the remote Wyoming dream." He sounded as if he was quoting from a leaflet, likely he was repeating Scott's words. "We could negotiate for fencing to partition, and sell off access rights. It would be a lot of money coming into the ranch."

Silence, and Jeff and Amy exchanged looks.

"Where will you go?" Amy asked.

"That's nothing to do with any of this. I've sent every dollar I could to back up this place, but there might be a time when I can't, and I need to be in a position where it's paying for itself."

In case something happens to me.

I'd made that decision yesterday, walking the land, seeing how it lay, and thinking about it as a future for at least one of the Lennox children, it just happened that it would be Rachel. I just had to explain what I was doing to her and get her to agree. Children need their mother, and there was no one left for me to disappoint now.

Jeff finally stood, bringing up Amy with him, and shook my hand.

"Okay," he said. "Okay."

Amy frowned at me, as if she was trying to figure out the trickiest kind of puzzle.

"Why you doing this?" she asked. She reached up to touch my face, but I caught her hand. What was it with people wanting to touch me? She used to show us kids affection when we were young, was the one who become something like a surrogate mom to us, but we'd never been close.

"It's done," was all I said. I hoped that in two words there was enough for her to stop asking questions. I went and found Rachel who was watching over a sleeping Laurie.

"We need to talk," I said, and sat on the floor with my back to the shut door.

She looked scared, glancing behind me at the door. "What's wrong? Are they here?"

"Who, Rachel? Who would be here, do you mean the cops, or do you think the others at the compound would find you? I need to know what I'm facing."

She shook her head, "No one leaves the place. No one will report what happened. They're survivalists, cut off from the outside."

"Can you be sure about that?" I needed to push her, and even that small question had her face crumpling.

"I think so." She hunched her shoulders, in tears.

"I need you to make me a promise."

She rested her other hand on her belly and turned a little to face me, wiping the tears from her face. "What promise?"

"If the cops come, and they could, you need to tell them it was me who shot Callum."

Her eyes widened and she shook her head mutely, gripping my hand.

"I need you to promise me," I insisted.

"Micah, no—"

"I have nothing to lose, but I will not let your children lose their mother. You hear me?"

"No."

"Laurie needs you, your baby needs you, I'm organizing it so you get this ranch, you make a home here, you do that for me, okay? But most of all, you tell them it was me that shot that bastard, that it was self-defense, but it was me that pulled the trigger."

She released her hold on my hand, and then reached up and I didn't flinch as she cupped my cheek and brushed a thumb over my cheekbone.

"I *wanted* to kill him for what he did to us," she said, and she was crying again, naked emotion in her voice. "You shouldn't suffer for his sins against me and Laurie."

I caught her hand, but not to pull her away, to hold it close, then I turned to press a kiss to her palm.

"Everything will be fine."

We hugged, the first time since the day she had left home, and she held me close. She cried and I rocked her, and somehow in those few minutes all the bad shit in our lives was gone.

And I felt like the hollow parts inside me were even more exposed than before.

SLEEP WAS a long time coming even though I was physically exhausted. I'd spent the day fixing the well cover, good honest work, and then slipped into duties with the horses as if I'd never been away.

At least I got to the point where I had a clarity of thought about my birthright. The parcel of land had to go if the rest of the Lennox Ranch was going to survive. As soon as I woke I would put a call in to Scott at his office, to say I wanted to negotiate on the land sale, and that was about as much as I could do.

And of course, because I had no control over my thoughts, Daniel was front and center as I dropped off.

I'd tried not to think of him, not in the time since we'd returned, but the regrets I had about what I'd done, and how I'd hurt the man I loved, were more than I could hold back.

He had the most beautiful eyes, and I'd fallen for him so hard.

So hard that I'd never experienced anything like it since.

The nightmares had stopped long ago, I'd become so used to them that I'd trained myself to wake up, like an instinct for self-preservation, but I wasn't sleeping. I spent the longest time staring at the ceiling, and then tossing from side to side. Two a.m. and I was still awake; I knew I'd pay for it come morning because my body clock was on ranch time. I turned over and focused on relaxing each muscle.

Tomorrow would come soon enough.

12

MICAH

When Scott arrived the next evening, I was prepared with a head full of figures and ideas. Most of them I had scribbled in my notebook and I had a minimum amount per acre that I would sell for. And questions; I had a lot of them.

Scott was always the young annoying kid who'd tagged along with me, Chris and Isaac, and nothing had really changed. He still talked too much, he still had a confident swagger, and hell, he was still sweet on Rachel.

I'd suggested meeting in town for the negotiation on selling the Lennox land, but he'd insisted on coming to the ranch, said he was "out that way". Considering the mountains were behind us and the ranch land beyond us stretched right to the interstate, I was sure he wasn't being truthful. Only I thought maybe it was because he wanted to be nosy.

But no. Evidently, he wanted an up close and personal look around in order to see Rachel.

Rachel wasn't playing ball, though. She'd disappeared

with a dozing Laurie to her room about ten minutes before he arrived and she wouldn't be coming out. She was exhausted, and Laurie was being extra clingy. Which meant that I was in the kitchen, with Scott, while Jeff and Amy hovered. I could've asked them to leave, but they were invested in this as well, so I let them stay. If Scott though that was odd he didn't comment, but then if he didn't stop peering past me toward the bedrooms he'd dislocate his neck, if that was even possible.

Probably not, but it sure seemed like he was trying hard.

After one intense stare at the hallway he returned to his coffee and more talking. Spread on the table were sketches and plans and notes, plus a draft contract for my consideration. Jeff edged closer to the table, checking out the plans, and I turned them a little so he could see.

"And the access road?"

That was the only thing I couldn't make out from the plan. The road from Whisper Ridge to the ranch was being dissected somehow, and the last thing any of us here wanted was for any kind of extra traffic crossing our place. Particularly if it was city people who didn't want the reality of a Wyoming ranch on their doorstep.

Scott pointed and explained his plans. Then he turned the maps back to me so I could make sense of them, and then it hit me, right in the solar plexus where this road veered from the main road. Right by the bridge at the edge of our land. No longer would the bridge and the end of the creek be part of Lennox land and I felt sick at the idea.

Remember, this is for Rachel, this is for the family.

"The bridge," I interrupted Scott's speech about improvements to the ranch road that would benefit us and the two words were enough to make him stop. I traced the map where the bridge was, and down to the names of the partners in Scott's development business. Each Sheridan sibling was there, and my hand shook a little as I traced Chris's name and then Daniel's.

Scott cleared his throat, "Chris wanted it included." He stared down at the map, and then up at me. He, Chris, and Daniel were so similar, the dark hair and eyes, and the solid-jaw-handsome that I'd fallen for with Daniel. "And we voted." He didn't look uncomfortable, just absolutely focused to the point that I think if I'd pulled out of the deal he wouldn't negotiate on the bridge. I honestly felt, at that moment, that this was a deal breaker for Sheridan Construction.

"What will you do?" I asked, emotion tightening my throat. I'd walked down there that morning and cleared the snow from Isaac's name. I spent some time talking to him, just as easily as I could at his grave, but with less chance of meeting anyone. If I turned my back to his name I could see the path that we'd taken down the hill in the car, imagine every last second until everything went wrong.

"Nothing," Scott said. "We voted that we wanted the bridge included in the sale, and we plan to put money in trust for upkeep."

"As a memorial to Isaac."

"Not just that but honoring a place that has touched a lot of lives."

I dipped my head then, stared unseeing at the maps, lost in my own bitter self-recriminations, wondering how many more of these gentle reminders I would have to face when I was back in Whisper Ridge.

"Yours included, Micah," Scott murmured. "Your life was changed that night."

I realized Jeff had vanished, along with Amy, and it was just me and Scott in the warmth of the kitchen. I found the courage to look up, expecting to see accusation on Scott's face. But his expression was compassionate.

I can never forget that night. I'm sorry for what happened to your brother. I'm sorry Isaac died. But I have to be here, and I have to make plans for my sister's future.

The words in my head remained unspoken and instead I went and refilled our coffee mugs and sat back down.

"Let's get this done."

Losing that bridge from our control meant nothing to me against what I had to do.

I'm so good at lying to myself.

When we were finished, and I had the draft contract in hand, with plans in my head that I'd approved of, he shook my hand, and did this awkward sideways hug. I didn't know how to react, but I sort of bumped his shoulder, and that was good enough.

"Uncle Micah?"

Laurie's small sleepy voice turned my attention, and I turned just as Rachel rounded the corner to capture him.

"I'm sorry," she said, and tried to catch him, but I beat her to it.

She'd just woken up, and she was sleepy, but also, in that light she appeared so fragile in one of the flowing tops I'd picked up for her. She'd pulled her hair back into its normal ponytail, but some of it had escaped and curled around her face. Rachel had been eating properly since we'd arrived, and even the week of food and warmth had changed her. She was as beautiful as I remembered her. I heard the small exhalation from Scott standing next to me.

“Rachel, it’s been so long, you’re looking well.” Scott extended his hand to her. I think he wanted to shake it, but I worried he might’ve wanted to hug her. I really wasn’t sure she would’ve been that good with a hug. He might have held her hand a little longer than Rachel was comfortable with, but she didn’t yank her hand back. "How are you?”

She smiled at him, and he grinned back, but I know I was the only who knew her well enough to see that the smile didn’t reach her eyes. “A little tired.” That was her standard reply, but he was nodding as if she’d read out an essay on her feelings.

He turned to me, “I’ll come back in a few days to talk through the contract.”

“I can come to town,” I said, even though I really wanted to avoid the place.

“No, I’d like to come back, get the lay of the land you know. Maybe, if it’s okay, I could bring your son a gift,” he was talking to Rachel again, but looking at Laurie who, weirdly enough, wasn’t hiding his face. “Do you like teddy bears?”

Silence. Laurie stared at his mom and then at me, and I rescued him.

“Jigsaws, he loves them, he’s doing simple ones meant for adults.” I was proud of Laurie and what he could do, and the words I spoke were heavy with that.

Scott smiled, and then with a tip of his imaginary hat at us all, he left.

But when the door shut, nothing had altered inside the house. Deciding to sell the land, seeing the plans and contracts meant nothing. Not until we signed and the money was safely in the bank.

Then everything would change.

THE CREW I'd assembled to work on the ranch bitched about the cold but worked hard. I was paying them as much as I could, borrowing from my meagre savings, and shoring up ranch finances so we could start making something of the place again.

There was money in a bank account, about half of what I'd sent in total, that was untouched, and that was enough to get some way through paying for the guys. What we really needed was the money from the sale, but even if it was the quickest contract negotiation ever, it would still take weeks.

The call to Henry Jr. was quick and to the point, and he loaned me money without asking any questions. The terms were short, the collateral was Jem I guess, but it was never spoken as being such.

He asked me if I was okay.

I just said yes, because, what else was I going to tell him? Then he pushed a little and I knew I had to explain enough so he could understand. He accepted family problems, he understood that I wanted to get Rachel settled into her new home.

He was my friend, my boss, and now my banker, I owed him that much.

Up since dawn, I'd worked side by side with the team, fixing the fences on the boundary where we would be selling the land. It was slow going, working in the snow, digging through frozen ground, using existing holes where we could, and making the best of a bad thing.

I had so many plans, if I was going to stick around. I could create the kind of place the K had—breeding good horses, training them, working to budgets and turning good profits. I wouldn't take their business, but I would have my own market and I could put everything back into the Lennox Ranch and it could be a place that people respected.

When we broke for coffee, steam from our breath fogging the air, and every other word a curse at the winter, I spent a short time planning in my head. Deciding where to situate things, like the training ring, better stables, converting part of the barn I was sleeping in into accommodation, so we could get a couple of permanent hands. We used to have that, when I was a kid.

By the time we were done for the day I'd resigned myself to all my plans never happening. This place could run with the money we made from the sale, maybe some cattle, some goats, hell, Laurie might like goats. Fix the old stables, contact people about boarding and training, find a hand who knew the ropes.

Then I could leave without feeling as if I was letting my sister down. On my way back to the ranch house, I stopped by the old barn that held the last thing of my dad's that I knew of.

The door was jammed shut with snow and earth, but I dug around it, broke the wood where the padlock was and pushed in. The interior was dark, but there was still enough light to see the car, or what was left of it. A tarpaulin had been laid over it as some point, but it must have been eaten away with age, or just slipped off. There was snow inside the car from the gaps in the roof.

"Your dad sent me up," Daniel called from the barn door. "He seems pissed, what did you do?"

"Nothing, he's always pissed." Even though all I wanted to do was kiss Daniel hello, I spent a few moments tugging at my overalls to cover the bruise forming on my collar bone. Courtesy of Dad and his best friend Whiskey. I wasn't ready to tell Daniel what an asshole Dad could be sometimes, but one day, if the things I felt inside me became something more, then I would share everything.

Daniel was a sight for sore eyes even if he was frowning at the car.

"Hell, what is this heap?

My overalls were covered in oil, and I grinned up at Daniel. "Dad's old car, he doesn't want it, said I could do what I want with it on my own time."

Daniel skirted the car once, and then ended up next to me.

You think you can fix this?" he sounded dubious, but he wasn't getting the point at all. I would never be able to fix this car, but I loved being away from the house. Since Rachel had left for college and it was just me and the old man, I needed somewhere to hide.

"It doesn't matter if I can't fix it, I just love messing with it."

"One day I'm going to get a Porsche," Daniel announced and patted the heap that was the rusting Mustang. "I'll be so rich it won't need fixing, ever."

"Can I drive it? Maybe I can be your chauffeur?"

Daniel pulled me close then, despite the oil, not caring that his skinny jeans would get covered in it. He'd been rocking the preppy look since he'd come back from college. In his last year at the University of North Carolina at Chapel Hill, he looked different to the boy I'd shared the summer with. His campus sweatshirt would be ruined, but the not caring about the mess appeared to extend to that as well.

He bent me back with the force of his kiss and I clung to him so we didn't fall ass-over-head onto the ground.

"Missed you," he growled and deepened the kiss. I clung to him until he moved us back and pushed me against the wall of the barn.

As soon as I had something stable to hold me up, I switched our positions, and it was me shoving Daniel where I needed him to be.

And I sunk to my knees. No one would come up here, Dad barely left the house anymore, and it was just me and Daniel.

I unzipped his tight-fitting jeans, cursed that the denim clung to his thighs, and he helped me to shimmy them down a little so I could get to my prize. With his boxers hooked under his balls I had his erection in my hand.

"Fuck, you're beautiful," I muttered, and kissed and licked until he begged to come. The power I had over this man, this gorgeous sexy man whom I loved, was enough to have my cock straining in my pants. I sucked him down and his erection bumped the back of my throat. I applied pressure and with a ragged groan he came hard, gripping my hair and pulling me away, finishing in my mouth. He grabbed me then, pulled me to stand, forced a hand into my loose pants and circled my cock, and then, kissing

messily, he brought me to an orgasm so hard I couldn't stand.

We ended up on the floor, side by side, staring at the car, holding hands and leaning into each other.

"I missed you so much," he repeated.

And I showed him how much I'd missed him by lacing my fingers through his and holding tight.

I love you, *was unspoken, but soon I would tell him.*

Soon.

I'D ALWAYS WANTED to drive, ever since I was a kid. Horses were my first love, but there was nothing like the speed of a car, and Dad had bought this when Mom was still alive. It was our project, mine and Dad's, much to Rachel's disgust when she was banned from there. It could be worth some money for parts, but what did I know. I was no expert on cars.

The times in the barn with Dad, before Mom died, had been some of my happier memories, but like the snow that melted in my hand as I pushed it from the steering wheel, they were vanishing to nothing.

The memories I had of me and Daniel here? They would never go, but they were fading with every passing day.

I attempted to pull the tarpaulin back over it, but there was a big chunk missing, and what the hell was I thinking anyway? Nothing could save this rusting old heap. I tugged at the door handle and it fell off, but I placed it carefully to one side, and found the loose screws. I put the screws with the handle and crouched next to the hole in the door. The only thing left there was rust, but if I sanded it back, welded, pushed, shoved, and cajoled.

Not that I had time to spare on messing around with a car. I had a ranch to fix up as best I could. Still, working on the car might've given me an excuse not to spend time in the house.

When I left I pushed the door back in place and wedged it shut with mud, stones, and snow, and promised myself to at least check-in on the car when I could.

Back at the house I took the contract and more coffee to the front room. Laurie came in with me, climbed onto my lap, and settled in for a hug. He fell asleep on me almost instantly, and I stroked his hair with one hand while checking the details in the contract. The Lennox Ranch was selling two hundred acres of its over three-thousand, and the price was more than fair. I knew, because I'd done research and I was happy that we weren't being ripped off. I hesitated only when I examined the map again and saw how the land I'd thought I'd always work, was being sliced up so dramatically to include the bridge.

I guess I had to trust that the Sheridan siblings, and Scott in particular, would care for the place where Isaac had died, and keep it for people to visit if they wanted to. Like Isaac's family. I wondered if they came to visit at all. Colleen Reynolds, had been a good person, and I remember seeing her in the hospital. She couldn't meet my eyes, and I didn't have the balls to go and talk to her. She wasn't in court when I received my year in prison, although her older children were, and they were happy to look right at me with condemnation in their expression.

No one else came except for Daniel, but he had to, given he was testifying.

Lying.

Rachel came into the room, searching for Laurie, and took the seat opposite me instead of waking the little guy.

"How you doing?" she asked.

I waved the contract. "About this?" I asked and I gave her a reassuring smile. "This is good for us. With the cash, you can hire workers, get a solid breeding program off the ground, board more horses. Laurie loves the horses, he'll be good with them."

"Good for you as well."

"Rachel, even if no one connects us to what happened, you know I'm not staying. You'll have a better start for you and the kids if I'm not here. People have long memories, and I promised I would never come back."

Rubbing her belly as she moved, she winced as she tried to ease herself back on the sofa. "That was nearly ten years ago now. Daniel can't make you leave."

She was wrong there. The chance of reconnecting to Rachel and being a real uncle to Laurie and the baby, was so real. But, the promise I made to the man I loved would always make me leave.

So, coward that I am, I changed the subject.

"I think I need to sign this."

I picked up the pen next to my coffee and smoothed out the page with my free hand and then, with no more thought than wanting my family safe and well, I signed.

13

DANIEL

THE NIGHTMARE HAD ME IN ITS GRIP. THE CORRIDORS I was walking down, then running through, were dark, twisty and never ending, and right in front of me was Julia, looking back and shouting my name.

When I woke, probably at the sound of my own yelling of her name over and over, I was covered in sweat — the sheets twisted around me so badly that I had to roll off the bed with them to get myself loose. I dropped my pajama pants, ripped off the soaked T-shirt and climbed straight into the shower. When I'd moved into the house, it was the first thing I'd wanted fixed. Way more than the decrepit forties kitchen, and a long way ahead of new carpets. There was nothing like standing in a shower, melting away the stress, giving me moments of silence in which I could think.

I didn't have the nightmares very often, just on nights when the days had been hard. Micah coming back into our lives equaled a very bad day, and even though it had been three days since I'd seen Rachel, and then him, I couldn't get his face out of my mind. The clock in the bathroom showed it was only five a.m. I wasn't due at work for another four hours, but I knew there was no point in trying to sleep. I stayed under the shower, for as long as I had hot water, and by the time I stepped out I was a wrinkled prune but I felt more awake and less panicked.

My counselor had said I should make a note of all my nightmares in a journal, but what was the point, it was always the same one. I just added it to my count, which was running at three times so far, this month. This was down from six in January.

Way to go, February!

Dressed, I stood in the middle of my ancient kitchen. When I'd bought the place, it had been for an absolute bargain, but the owner, Old Man Henderson, had lived in the house, man and boy, and had died at ninety-seven. He'd bathed in a metal tub in front of the fire. And evidently, he'd existed with a small countertop fridge, a one ring stove, and a sink suspended between two crumbling cabinets. Scott had persuaded me this was a bargain. He'd spent an entire morning explaining about equity and other things I ignored.

Because I'd loved this house since I was a kid.

It was the haunted house. Every town has one; a creepy house with an overgrown garden and an owner that no one ever saw. As kids, Chris and I would dare each other to knock and run, and I'd always pretended to be scared, but hell if I was. The place fascinated me, all sharp angles and ivy that covered the walls, with a garden that wasn't so much overgrown as incredibly full. I could hide in that garden, and Old Man Henderson never came out and told me to leave. Maybe he'd never even known that I would sneak in at the end of his garden and sit in among the bushes to read. I like to think that he'd known, but that he hadn't minded.

The irony was that this garden, the one I'd worked hard to tame now, was the same place in which I'd first had feelings for Micah.

"I DARE you to go into the garden."

Chris stared right at me. My brother was an asshole. I loved the Henderson place, but it was dark. There was a maze of old trees and bushes that were horrific shapes in the dark, holding horror and held all kinds of dreadful things.

"I went in there last week," I defended.

Micah hovered between us, always the one to try to calm the sibling shit. He was Chris' best friend and spent so much time at our house he was like a brother. He'd been quiet recently, but losing his mom was hard, and even though he appeared to bounce back, this summer he'd been withdrawn and edgy.

"We don't have to make him go in there." Micah said, and peered into the darkness.

Of course, Micah saying that had the opposite effect.

"Triple dog dare you," Chris said and laughed at me, and I was abruptly determined to show my little brother I wasn't scared. I was sixteen and I was no coward.

The branches snagged my jacket, the leaves tangled in my hair, but with absolute focus I made it to the tree in the center of the garden, high on the fact I'd done it, and had not been eaten by whatever monsters lived in the snarled undergrowth. There was noise behind me, the trampling of footsteps and I assumed a pose of not caring I was there, even though my heart beat a thousand times a minute. I expected Chris, but it was Micah who appeared, waving his flashlight to find me.

"What are you doing?" I whispered loudly, and snatched the flashlight from him, pointing the beam at the ground. "What if old man Henderson looks out and sees us."

"I'm not scared," Micah fronted, and puffed out his chest. He was a skinny twelve-year-old and I could see he was lying.

I stepped closer, pointed the flashlight under my chin and made a grimace with my face, then deepened my voice. "You should be scared, Micah Lennox." He stepped away from me, tripped on a root and fell on his ass, and I couldn't help laughing. I helped him to stand and expected him to move away but he didn't.

"There's a lot of things I'm scared of; monsters ain't one of 'em."

He sounded so grown-up, way ahead of any of the shit that Chris came out with.

"Whatever," I laughed and walked back the way I came, hearing him follow. We almost made it to the road, just a few more bushes to clamber through.

"Daniel, can I ask you something?"

"Yeah," I didn't even think about it, I was concentrating on not falling on my ass.

"How old were you when you knew you were gay?"

THE MEMORIES RUSHED AT ME, and that led to remembering that this was the first place I'd kissed Micah.

When we'd been drinking, me at twenty-two, Micah just turning nineteen and deciding that he wanted to experiment with me.

Or at least I thought it was an experiment.

But it had become more over that summer before I left for my last year at UNC-Chapel Hill. Much more.

I rubbed my chest, where the knot of anxiety still threatened to return, and thought back to the more innocent days when a tangle of bushes hid my reading, and my loving. He'd lost his virginity with me, uncomfortably, in the tangled quarter acre of plants and bushes; three months of kisses had become too much not to take it further. Even though that memory existed, it was one of many, and when Scott had told me the house was on the market, I'd jumped at the chance to own it.

My counselor would likely have said it was because I wanted to punish myself or some such crap, but I just loved the garden.

Of course, as soon as I'd moved in, I took an axe to the tree that we'd gotten off against. I took out every ounce of anger on that poor thing, until there was nothing more than a pile of broken branches and a hacked off trunk. I bet if I'd told my counselor back in Charlotte that, I would've gotten a raised eyebrow and a soft shake of the head. Not that she would have had a chance to tell me anything when I refused to go back.

"Don't give into the anger," the short gray-haired woman had said to me, tapping her folder, and daring me with an expression that willed me to agree.

I clenched my fists and my right hand ached from where I'd punched Micah. I'd always wondered what I would do if I ever saw Micah again.

Would I hit him? Or hug him close and tell him I'd missed him?

Maybe before the incident at the hospital in Charlotte, I would have chosen the latter, but my head was screwed, which was a deceptively simple way to wrap up my anxieties and the PTSD. Hitting him had won out. My hand still ached, and I thought maybe I'd given myself a hairline fracture in there somewhere. I'd handled worse.

The kitchen clock, a small thing shaped like a tomato that Mark had bought me for Christmas, told me it was six. There wasn't any point in hanging around.

I might as well go into work and get ahead of my day. No point in standing at the window staring out at the garden and thinking on things I shouldn't.

Wrapped up in my thickest coat against the Wyoming winter cold I left the house, locked the door, stepped back and looked up at it. Three beds, no baths, fuck-all in the way of a kitchen, an untamed jungle for a garden.

I loved this place.

There had been more snow overnight, not much, but enough to cover the ice beneath it on the sidewalk, and it made walking a little tricky until I got used to it. Muscle memory was a thing. I'd used to be able to run on the icy sidewalks, but I'd become soft in Charlotte with all that sunshine. The clinic was empty, and I locked the door behind me when I went inside.

First order of the day? Coffee. Second? Sorting through the mail that had accumulated on my desk. Coffee in hand, I moved from room to room, lost in thought, and soaking in the familiar scents and sights. My dad's office was the mirror to mine, but it held thirty years of memories and assorted paraphernalia. From his diplomas on the wall to his signed Clapton guitar, the walls had barely an inch to spare. Mom was the kind of person who hated clutter and their house was neat and mess-free; I think Dad liked this place because it was his and he could have as much clutter as he wanted. I remember watching him work. Not with patients, but scribbling notes, opening huge books full of amazing diagrams and lists of things with long important sounding names. I used to be the only one of the five of us that *wanted* to sit on the chair next to his desk and watch him work.

He was the reason I was a doctor, and I was always going to come home to take my place here.

I'd had to speed up the timetable for the move, but Dad was appreciative. He and Mom wanted to take time for themselves now that Mark was away at college.

My desk was clearer. I didn't need the big old medical books, my information was digital and available online, and my certifications were propped up against the wall to one side. I settled at the desk and ran through all the correspondence, and I hadn't even realized I'd drifted into daydreams until I took a sip of coffee and it was stone cold.

I'd been thinking about the promises Micah and I had made each other when we were young, of him making the Lennox Ranch the biggest and best, and me being the town doctor. Of maybe making a life for ourselves here. Stupid, childish, ambitions.

He'd been wild, his mom gone, his dad distant, there'd been no one to tell him to stop. He took what he wanted and I had been the focus for a long time. I was eighteen, he'd been three years younger, but he was relentless. He kissed me, pushed me, and I was weak against his wildness.

"You're early."

Chloe was standing in the doorway holding two mugs of coffee.

"Is one of those for me?" I smiled up at her when she passed it over.

"Morning to you too," she teased.

I sipped the dark bitter brew and imagined it trickling through my veins. The damn stuff kept me going after a shit night like last night.

"If you weren't already married…" I said the same thing every time, and she always had the same reply.

"If only I was a few years younger…"

The day was uneven, busy in the morning, and then quiet in the afternoon, and when I stopped around four, I ran through my list of house visits. That was what I liked about being a small-town doctor, the ability to form relationships with patients, to know the people behind the illnesses. My first stop was to Amanda Ribbin, a few days past her ninety-second birthday, and complaining of headaches. I think what she wanted most was company. I stayed for cake and coffee, and listened to her talk about her children and great grandchildren. I even looked at some pictures of a new addition to the family, the next generation of Ribbins.

Then it was on to the garage. The owner, Bill, was one of my regulars. There was a lot of things wrong with him, diagnosed with MS in his forties, some ten years ago. One thing was worrying me, a recent blood test had shown higher sugar levels than I would've liked, and I gave him dietary advice, a friendly ear, and helped him to work out a figure on his books that was giving him cause for frustration. His wife appeared as I was leaving. She ran the garage below, and she seemed tired. I know the business was busy, but money was tight, add in the medical issues and I think the burden on this family was great. I stopped to talk to her, and then I was done except for one last visit–the one I'd been dreading.

Rachel.

I REVERSED into a space just beyond the front yard at the Lennox Ranch. Part of me was convinced I'd have to make a quick exit, and how sad was that? I couldn't get any closer anyway, the yard itself was a mix of snow, broken dirt and choking weeds—it had been for a very long time. When Micah had been there he'd worked long hours around school to keep it going, hell, they'd had a couple of hands back then. Then everything had happened with his dad, and finally, the accident, and along with Micah leaving, the ranch had fallen into disrepair.

I know that they boarded two horses. They belonged to people in Whisper Ridge. They used to board more, but I imagine two was as much as Jeff could handle on his own. This ranch was land rich, but what the hell they used for money, apart from whatever Micah sent home, I didn't know.

"Afternoon Doc," Jeff said and tipped his hat. He was walking past the car to the stables and I nodded back.

"Afternoon."

That was as far as my interaction with Jeff Reynolds ever went. There was something about him that I didn't understand. He had this way of staring at a man as if he could see through him. Now, Amy, she was an easy person to talk to, normally. She answered the door, after I'd steeled myself for Micah to open it. I had no idea what I would say if I saw him.

Rachel seemed a hundred times better. We went into her small room, her son in tow. The bruises I'd seen on both of them were fading now, but the little guy wasn't interested in me. He just wanted to hold his momma's hand and hide behind the long blond hair that he pulled forward. He was underweight for his age, and it didn't help he was also quite tall for a five-year-old, but he was healthy, even if he was quiet.

I listed to the baby's heartbeat, the steadiness of it reassuring.

Rachel looked at me and I held her gaze for a short while until staring into her eyes, so much like her brother's it freaked me out.

"Are you taking some vitamins now?"

"Micah got me everything I need."

"And an appointment with the midwife?"

"Not yet."

I made a mental note to get our community midwife here if she didn't hurry and get an appointment. I couldn't make her see a midwife, but jeez, she needed to be checking things were okay.

"Micah bought me some things for the baby," she said, clearly trying to change the subject, and pointed to a small pile of clothes and diapers.

I didn't want to talk about Micah, but the patient came first. "That's nice," I said, acutely aware of how lame I sounded.

Laurie took that moment to climb off his mom and sit

on the bed next to her, leaning on her belly as if he was listening for his sister or brother. I was concentrating on how cute that picture was when I realized she was talking to me.

"Sorry?" I prompted.

"I just said that Micah is a good man, don't judge him by what happened all those years ago."

The words were heavy with meaning.

I didn't know what to say. I didn't know the man he had become, only the wild young man he'd been then, the one who'd said he was in love with me. But, some things I couldn't get past.

I changed the subject. "I'd like you to come down to the clinic—"

"I'd rather we see each other here," she interrupted. "Easier for everyone."

"I'd like you to rethink that."

"No. I'm staying here."

"You have a responsibility towards your unborn baby and getting the right care," I warned.

She laid a hand on her belly and pulled Laurie closer, "We'll be fine."

I bit back the rest of my words and made a mental note to visit again in a week. Finished, I left the house, thanking all who would listen that I hadn't seen Micah, and feeling this side of smug that I'd managed that without trying.

Micah stood by my car. Bundled up in his coat he was very definitely waiting for me, intending to say something.

"Micah," I acknowledged.

"She won't go to town," he said, without introduction.

"I know. If it's a matter of insurance, we can find ways around that."

He stiffened. "We can pay for what we need to," he said, pride making his tone defensive. "I told her she needs to get medical care; she won't listen to me. But if *you* tell her, then you can *make* her go."

"No, *Micah*, I can't make your sister do anything she doesn't want to unless I feel she needs to be in a hospital. She's well, and I will organize a midwife visit."

"She won't go because she's worried what people might say. Laurie won't leave her side and she doesn't want any trouble that he could see." He paused and looked down at the snow, kicking at a stone. "The kid's seen enough in his life."

Of course, people in town would maybe stare, and point, some of them might even go up to Micah and confront the ghosts of the past. By extension his sister could well face the same kind of issues. I wished I could've told her, and Micah, that it would all be okay.

"I can't *make* your sister go to town; I'll come to her unless I think she needs to be in the hospital."

"Thank you," Micah said.

I shivered as a gust of icy wind whirled around us, and one-handed, I pushed up the collar on my jacket. It got stuck on my scarf and for a moment I thought I saw Micah reach to help me, but I must have been seeing things. There was no way he would've done anything like that, and I wouldn't have let him even if he had.

We stared at each other in the cold, at an impasse on what to say next. I should've gotten in the car and left, but I felt like maybe he had something on his mind. So, I waited, half afraid of what he might say.

"You're a doctor now. You always said you would be one day."

That wasn't a question, more of a statement. I left the silence between us long enough so it got awkward. Leaving it wasn't deliberate, I was just lost for how to respond.

"What did you do, after you got out of…?" I shrugged because it was too cold to use my hands to indicate a word I didn't want to use.

"Prison. You *can* use the word Daniel." He moved even deeper into his coat. "You want to get a coffee somewhere in town to talk?"

"No," I said without thought. I did *not* want to be in a warm place talking to Micah, having to confront the feelings that swelled inside me whenever I saw him. I walked around him and got into the car, and as far as I was concerned this was my cue to get the hell out of Dodge.

He followed me and ended up standing way too close.

"I missed you," he murmured. "I want you to know that."

I shuffled backward in the snow, the solid car at my back. He stepped forward, and he got into my personal space, but instead of being freaked out, I didn't move at all, and didn't feel the familiar claustrophobic panic that normally gripped me. I waited for the shoe to drop, for Micah to do something.

"I missed you too," I went for honesty, but it came with a caveat. "But not for a long time."

He reached out and pressed a bare hand to my cheek. I refused to turn my head and kiss his palm. But I wanted to.

"What we had was amazing," Micah said and closed the space between us. The press of his lips to mine was gentle, and I had plenty of time to pull back. To shove him. Curse him. I didn't do any of that, I settled into the soft barely-there kiss and I wanted to lean on his hand. He didn't deepen the kiss, and he moved away a little, running his thumb over my bottom lip. "So amazing," he repeated.

Then, when the feeling of the kiss subsided, and the panic gripped, I scrambled into the car and shut the door on him. If he was any kind of normal human being he would get the message and go away.

Micah opened the passenger door and climbed in.

"What the hell?" I asked.

"You wanted to know what I did after prison, so I'll tell you."

"I'm cold."

"Start the engine, let it warm up, put the heating on, and I'll tell you what you wanted to know."

"I was just being polite," I snapped.

Micah wasn't moving, whatever I said. The engine turned smoothly and we waited a little while before switching on the heat, and finally after a few minutes of awkward silence the car warmed and Micah pushed back his hood.

The first thing I saw was the split lip. It was healing nicely, but seeing it laid a ton of guilt on top of the claustrophobia I felt in the too-small car. I pushed back my hood and faced front and center.

"After they let me out, I tried to find work. There's not much out there for someone with a record, particularly stealing of property and reckless endangerment. I did what I could, and finally ended up working at the height of the summer on this ranch called the Triple-K, just outside Denver. I'm a hard worker, knew my way around horses, and they gave me a job, and in seven years I became an investor, training horses and taking a cut of profit, and everything I could afford I sent back here. So that sums up where I was."

I wanted to tell him that I didn't want to know, but I would've been lying. Deep inside me, in my heart, that still held some connection to Micah, I desperately needed to know, more than anything, that he'd been okay.

I unzipped my coat, it was getting unbearably warm and my breathing was shallow. When that wasn't enough I slipped it off, and nearly hit Micah in the face again. He watched me as I wriggled. My arm got stuck and he held the material so I could tug myself out. The cool air that not even my car heater could dispatch fanned my face and for a few moments I thought I'd be okay.

"What's wrong?" Micah asked, but his voice was distant. I couldn't tell him but I knew damn well for sure I was about to have a fucking panic attack. I pulled the sweater away from my throat and reached over to lower the temperature, but I was fumbling, and Micah did it for me. Then I felt his hand on my shoulder, moving to stroke my hair. I wanted to tell him to leave me alone, but my body was telling me otherwise.

In the end I closed my eyes and sat as still and as small as I could and focused on the rhythmic movement of his hand and worked through the steps that Devin had given me in our most recent counseling session. Micah was talking as well, but I wasn't listening to what he was saying.

Breathe.

When I finally felt it was okay to open my eyes, Micah moved back and away and kept his hands in his lap.

"I feel like I need to talk to you," he announced, and then waited for me to answer.

"I don't think it's a good idea," I was antsy to go.

"Daniel, please, just one conversation? I don't have much time, I'll be leaving soon, and I want to clear the air."

What could Micah possibly have to say that needed saying? There was nothing left to cover. I shot him a glance and I could see his white-blond hair and pale eyes in the light from the porch. It gave him an exotic, otherworldly look, as if he didn't belong on a ranch in Wyoming at all.

"I loved you," he said, and just those three words rocked my world.

"What the hell?" I'd heard what he said, but maybe I'd misunderstood.

"I loved you for a very long time, from when I was twelve, and I know I was only nineteen when we ended up together, but I knew you were it for me."

"Micah—"

"No, you have to listen to me. I never stopped." He reached out and pressed a hand to my chest. "I know there's no chance for us now, that there's been no chance for a long time, but I want you to know that *whatever* happens now, I never stopped."

I pushed his hand away and he didn't fight me.

"You don't get to say that shit," I began calmly, even though panic threatened again.

He shrugged, as if he was done, not willing to talk about what he'd just said.

That made me angry, and frustrated, and all messed up again. I wasn't ready to let him have the last say in this.

"You're leaving then? What about your sister, huh? What about your nephew who is scared of his own shadow? Are they going with you?" I was irrationally angry at how easy it seemed for him to leave.

"No, they have a home here, and I have work in Denver."

"Probably a good thing. Chris will never forgive you. I never loved you, and your sister and nephew will be fine without you."

The fierce heat of panic gripped me again. *Jesus, I am losing control here. I want to hurt him.* I started the car and waited for him to get out, but evidently, he wasn't done.

"I read about what happened to you in Charlotte," he said. "I'm sorry for your loss." He leaned over to me, pressed a kiss to my cheek, and then let himself out the car. "Night, Daniel."

I drove away as soon as he was out, without a backward glance, but I knew one thing for sure; I was certain to have the nightmare again tonight.

14

MICAH

I WATCHED DANIEL LEAVE, WAITING UNTIL THE RED OF THE tail lights vanished into the whirling snow, and still I stood there in the cold.

I couldn't believe I'd kissed him. I had no right to do that, but in that single moment I felt as if I could touch him and that somehow the last nine years would magically vanish. Then stroking his hair when he had his panic attack, and, god, kissing his cheek.

What the hell had I been thinking?

Chris will never forgive you. I never loved you, and your sister and nephew will be fine without you. His words carved into me because I knew them to be true. Or at least I'd convinced myself that Chris hated me, and that there was no way Daniel had ever loved me.

The last one, about Laurie being better off without me? Was that true? I was good with kids, and Laurie was a little-me. I desperately wanted him to like me, to turn to me when he needed something. I didn't want him hating me. Hell, the selfish side didn't want him to be fine without me.

Of course, Daniel had never really loved me, I'd got used to that idea, otherwise he wouldn't have told me to go nine years ago. We would have fought, and kicked, and screamed at each other, but at the end of it, we'd have worked our way through if the love had been real on both sides. Maybe not as partners, but at least with some kind of relationship, like friendship, or something mutually respectful.

No, he'd cut me out of his life and said I was nothing to him. That wasn't evidence of the love I thought he had for me.

Childish, stupid infatuation, was all it had been, and one-sided when it came to being in love.

And what about Chris? Why should he ever forgive me? I'd written to him when I was in prison. He and Isaac had been my best friends, but he'd never replied with anything, not even hate.

It felt as if everything was closing in, as if the cops were just a mile away, coming for me, taking me away from there. I wasn't done yet. I needed to fix things on the ranch, put procedures in place, sell the damn land to help finance. I had to make it right for Rachel, Laurie and the baby. Daniel was professional with Rachel, didn't give any sign that the anger or distrust he felt for me was ever going to be visited on her or her kids.

If Daniel said Chris didn't forgive me, then what if Chris hated me, and held onto that hate for Rachel?

Hell, I needed to make things right with Chris before I left.

But what if the cops were right there, looking into a murder at the Brothers' compound.

"Are you coming in?" Rachel called from the door and startled me. I turned to face her with a pasted smile on my face, then moved into the warmth of the kitchen. There was dinner on the table, some kind of stew that smelled amazing, and piles of potatoes in a large bowl in the middle. I saw they'd set a place for me, but I felt sick, and I couldn't eat right now.

"Where does Chris live?" I asked my aunt as soon as I was inside. She had her back to me, stirring the stew, but I could see her shoulders stiffen at the question.

"He won't want to see you." she said.

Even though I knew that was likely true, I wanted to defend my question. "You don't know that he won't see me."

She made a noise of disbelief.

"Jesus, Amy," I snapped. "Will you give it a rest, I'm about done with your shit."

I'd never spoken to her like that, hell, never spoken to anyone that way. But I was done with everything I'd just had thrown at me in the car, and the fact I was sleeping outside, and when I was in the house all I got was anger and misery. This kind of environment wasn't good for Laurie and I needed everything to be finished and put away. Amy deliberately placed the wooden spoon on the rest and braced her hands on the sides of the stove, not facing me, not giving any sign of what she was feeling.

"You left, Micah," she said. Then she turned to face me and I saw grief and temper in her expression. "Rachel went to college, you never came back after prison, and you left me with your dad, and I had to deal with everything. The ranch, your dad's drinking, the hell that the Lennox Ranch had become. Do you know it was me that found your dad the day he died?"

"No, I didn't."

"You don't know anything of what we had to do. I came into the house, and it was quiet, but there was a smell, like iron, and there was all this blood. You know what I saw?" She moved closer and lowered her voice. "He was in the bathroom, clutching a picture of your mom. His brain was dead, his face gone, and there was so much blood. He'd tried to cut his wrists, made a mess of his arms, and when that didn't work he blew his face away. I found that, and you left me to deal with everything leading to that."

Her voice hitched, and for a moment I thought she might cry. I hadn't known who had found him dead, just that the man who'd hated me and Rachel was gone. I'd mourned him in my own way, with a fifth of whiskey and a toast to the horses I'd been taking care of. The call hadn't been from Amy, but Jeff, who couldn't get the words out and hung up on me once he was sure I had the *fucking message.*

"I'm sorry, but I couldn't have known what he was going to do."

She looked up at me, furious, "I don't care why you didn't come back, but you don't get to stand here in my kitchen and tell me you are sick of my shit." The word sounded wrong coming from her; she never cursed. My defensiveness vanished as quickly as it had arrived.

"I wish I hadn't gone. I'm sorry. Maybe if I'd stayed I could have dealt with Dad's problems as a man, maybe I could have stopped Rachel from staying away. Maybe we could all have been home and it could have been perfect. I don't know. But I do know I'm sorry that I left you to deal with it all."

It was a grand speech and I thought maybe she'd have something to say in response, call me on my bull, or have an opinion. Instead she turned back to the dinner she was preparing.

"Chris is down on Trent, drives a pickup, blue, third place from the end."

I pulled on my coat again then left the house before anyone could add any more doubt to the already significant pile I carried around with me. Amy shouting at me had nudged me out of my own head, and unraveled one of the close knotted threads of guilt inside me. Apologies for what I had and hadn't done were cathartic, but I doubted that my issues with Amy were all finished with. Life and relationships aren't easy and I'd had years to get used to that.

Getting into town was a challenge. My old truck slipped and slid on the new snow, and there was no doubt in my mind that it wouldn't take much more for the Lennox Ranch to be snowed in. Town itself was mostly clear and I cruised through the center, looking for the first time at the streets I'd used to call home.

Some shops were still there, like Bridges Mercantile. Owned by Nigel Bridges and started by his daddy, the mom and pop store had aged badly, but the light was on, and I saw someone walking in. Used to be I could get anything I wanted from Bridges, from one cent candy to remote control cars. I wondered if it was still the same, or if things had moved on enough that I wouldn't recognize them. There was a coffee shop where the diner used to be, but a new diner had appeared at the end of road near the boarded-up beauty parlor. I'd had my first haircut in that parlor, and had hated every minute of it, made to stare in a mirror at myself. After that visit, Mom buzz cut my hair at home, then after she'd died I did it myself. It was a style I'd kept for a long time. I ran a hand through my hair, it was getting longer now, and if I wasn't careful I'd end up looking like Laurie.

I turned off Main, headed for Trent Drive, named for the man who'd settled here and made this town at the feet of the Wind River Mountain Range, or as the locals called it, the Winds. I found Chris' place easily. If the truck hadn't been a giveaway, then the ramp to the front door was another clue. I killed the engine a few houses past his, sitting in the dark until the cabin was cold enough that I either left to go to Chris's house, or turned the engine back on and left.

THE FLAMES CREPT CLOSER as I managed to free Isaac from his belt. The car had landed at a crazy angle in the creek and the water lapped at his face. I had to get him out first, but I could hear Chris screaming, and the heat was worse. Finally, I got Isaac away, he was limp, unconscious, but there was no blood.

That had to be a good sign.

I scrambled back down the incline, and climbed the car, the metal hot to touch, the flames orange, and Chris covered in so much blood. He had stopped screaming, was silent, but I pulled and yanked him out, he was stuck, the fire burning his jacket around his neck, and I slapped at it until it stopped, and somehow, I dragged him away next to where Isaac lay.

He fell on me, slippery with blood, and I grappled for my phone, calling 911.

It was only when I had the guys on the line, telling me they would be there soon, that I saw Chris' face, burnt and red.

And only after I dropped the phone to the grass, that I saw the horror that was what was left of Chris' leg.

HE'D BEEN in a coma past my trial, and then when I was locked away, he hadn't visited. I'd written to him from prison, so many times, but there had been no reply from him and it was obvious that he'd wanted nothing to do with me.

I couldn't even think about when I last saw him, otherwise I'd get in the car and drive back to the ranch.

This was for Rachel; making things right for her and the kids.

Shoulders back, and with a crushing pressure on my chest, I went up to the front door and knocked.

15

MICAH

Of course, the man who opened the door wasn't the nineteen-year-old boy of my memory, and words fled from my mind at the sight of him. He looked shocked, his dark hair tousled, his eyes owlish behind glasses, and his mouth falling open. I could see the scarring on his face, the twist of burn marks that went from smooth to jagged, from his left cheekbone to his jaw. I remember putting my hands over the fire eating at his skin, suffocating flames so that he didn't die. I remember his screams, and they had never ever left me.

My confidence fled, and it was probably telegraphed in the way I stumbled back. I caught myself at the last moment and I swear I saw a flash of sadness in his eyes. Then it vanished and in its place was a cool welcome.

Chris leaned back from the door, opening it wide. "Jeez, if it isn't Micah Lennox. Wondered when you'd finally get here."

"Chris," was all I could say.

"Come in," he said and turned to walk the hall to the

kitchen. He had rails that ran the length of the wall both sides, using them to move fast. I glanced down at his right leg. He was wearing cutoff sweats and I saw the stump. Seeing the results of what I had done was worse than any horror I could imagine, and shame curled inside me.

I did that to him.

"Don't just stand there letting the cold in," Chris called back. I followed him in, shutting the door, and wondered what the hell to do next. "Take your coat and shoes off, I'll make coffee, or do you want beer?"

"I'm sorry, I'm not sure what I'm doing here, I know I promised Daniel that I wouldn't come back, but I'm here, and, fuck, I just wanted to see you."

"Coffee or beer?" he repeated, ignoring my impassioned speech and the apology along about being back in Whisper Ridge along with it.

"Chris—"

"Choose a damn drink, Micah! It's not a difficult question."

"Coffee," I said, and then cleared my throat as my voice caught.

I toed off my shoes, and hung my coat on the hook, then padded down the hallway after him, passing the wall of photos in mismatched frames, and refusing to check if there were any from before the accident. I already had clear images in my mind of what Chris used to look like, and the memories of him burning, of his leg shattered in the accident.

And his screams.

I hovered outside the kitchen, with no idea what to do, or say, or why the hell I was even here.

You're here for Rachel. You want to make sure he's going to welcome her to town.

"Coffee," Chris held the coffee just out of my reach and reaching for it had me stepping into the small kitchen. In a smooth move, that belied the fact he was on one steady leg, he slipped past me and took my place at the door. Abruptly, I was trapped in the small space with no way out.

"Thank you," I offered, even as every muscle in me tensed for flight. He didn't move from his spot.

"Start from the beginning. What do you want?" he asked, not accusing, only curious.

"It's about Rachel, I need to ask you something, and I know it's me asking you for a courtesy, but can you look past that and see that this is all for Rachel."

God that sounded so ridiculous. We had such a huge *thing* sitting between us, festering like an open sore, and I was telling him I was there asking him for a freaking *favor*?

"Jesus, Micah, calm down."

But I couldn't calm down, I was a mess, and he could see that as well as I could feel it.

"I wrote to you," I blurted. Letters from prison, begging, pleading, then guilt ridden, and it seemed like a good place to start with everything I needed to say.

"I know." He leaned against the doorjamb and crossed his arms over his chest. I realized he didn't have a drink at that point. Feeling at a disadvantage, I placed my coffee on the counter next to where he'd left his.

"I just wanted you to know…"

"That you were sorry," Chris said. "I didn't need to read your letters to know they would say you were sorry."

"Oh." How did I answer that? He stared right through me and I felt hot, ashamed, angry, and sad, all at the same time. The anger was entirely focused back on myself.

"I hated you," he said with feeling. I looked for revulsion in his expression, or anger, but weirdly enough, he was calm, focused, and held my gaze.

"I'm so sorry." What else could I say? I *was* sorry. For taking the keys and the car, for agreeing with my friends to get in the damn thing and try to jump the bridge. I was more than wretched, I was consumed with remorse and I always would be. It was a blackness that never seemed to ease, however hard I tried to tell myself that I was a stupid kid.

I'd been nineteen. Old enough to know better than to take stupid chances.

"God, I hated you so much," Chris shook his head.

"I deserved it."

He ignored me and pressed on. "Every day I woke up to pain, I wished I could die, I begged to go back to the crash and make you leave me in the car."

"What the hell?" The car had been alight, flames licking and crawling toward us, "You would have been burned alive. I wouldn't have left you to burn." The horror at the thought of it, took my breath. I would have gone into that car even if it was just about to explode, I'd have done anything to get Chris or Isaac out.

"You don't understand. I woke up in the hospital and my leg was gone, and everything I'd ever wanted was gone. My life was gone. Girlfriend, you remember Susie? Gone. The pain, hell, I've never felt anything like it, my face was scarred, the concussion, and then the worst of it, the phantom pains when I would wiggle my toes to try and there was nothing there. You know what arrived just after the accident? When I was still in the coma? A letter requesting my attendance at baseball trials. And I was in bed, and I couldn't move, and the pain was unbearable. Mom read the letter to me when I first woke up and she sobbed through the whole thing. I loathed you and I wanted desperately to die. Did you know I even took pills, overdosed on pain killers Dad had brought home for his back? I tried to end the pain and the PT and the endless blackness of my future. I would have succeeded as well, only Daniel found me."

Every ounce of energy left me and I slumped back against the counter. "Jesus—" I didn't think I had the energy to fight back against that. It was only what I'd expected and deserved.

But Chris hadn't finished, and I steeled myself for more.

"I told myself it was all on you." He blew out a breath. "I didn't open the letters because I didn't want to read your apology. You nearly killed me, and I lost my leg. It was *all your fault.*"

"I know. Jesus, I know."

"No, you don't know anything, because I was *wrong*, Micah. And guess what? My family wouldn't *let* me die, they pulled me back, and I slowly began to make sense of what had happened. An accident, Micah, it was just a lousy accident, and it wouldn't have happened if I'd just let up on goading you to prove yourself to me."

"You didn't—"

He wouldn't let me talk.

"I still didn't open your letters, because even though everyone went on a one-man mission to make sure I saw you had paid for what happened, it wasn't true. How could you ever pay for something that wasn't your fault? *Fuck.* It wasn't your fault."

"It was, *I* took the car and drove it, killed Isaac, destroyed your life," I snapped, because it *was* my burden, everything was *my* doing. Who the hell was Chris to tell me what I should or shouldn't feel?

"Do you remember that night?" Chris asked patiently.

"Of course, I do." Every. Single. Moment.

"We were kings of the world." Chris said, and he was lost in the memories. "Three best friends on Christmas Eve, nothing could touch us, and when you turned up with the car, Isaac and me were desperate to be part of everything you did. We were always together, you remember that."

I was glad the counter was holding me up. Chris unfolded his arms and his hands were clenched into fists. I wanted him to hit me just like Daniel had done. Maybe then I'd begin to find some kind of peace.

"I remember."

"You jumped the Whisper Ridge Creek at the first go, and landed flat on the wheels, and it was the best feeling in the world. I was high on the sheer love of it."

"Yeah."

Chris smiled then, "I told you to go again."

I nodded. Chris had always been most vocal of the three of us, a live-wire, destined for greatness, maybe even playing for our beloved Chicago Cubs one day. He'd be a millionaire, and get a jet, and fill the jet with girls, and some extra guys just for me. He'd said so, and he was always right. And that night he'd told me to go again. But that didn't mean I had to do it.

"And do you remember Isaac was shouting at you to keep going, and I looked back at him, and he was sitting in the back, grinning like a loon. Drunk off his ass, and so damn happy."

"Chris please—"

"Then you went on reverse as far as was possible, one handed, as fast as you could, and we were invincible, Isaac laughed so loud and so hard I thought he'd piss himself, and you slammed your foot to the floor and we'd never gone so fast."

I felt nauseous, desperate for Chris to stop talking. I remembered every sickening second of speeding along the side road toward the broken bridge with the absolute certainty that I'd hit the wood just right and we'd leap the stream that separated Lennox and Sheridan land again. I'd just done it once, it was nothing, a three-foot jump that we used to make every day on our bikes when we were smaller, and the car rumbled and growled down the road to the target. We hit the wood dead center, and it felt just like before. We flew.

God, how we flew.

Ripping my focus free of those memories, my ability to stand fled and I slid down the cabinet until I sat on the floor, my legs pulled up and my arms wrapped around them.

Chris made a noise. Was he laughing? How could he laugh when he recalled what had happened? Was he laughing at how pathetic I was, curled into myself on the floor? I looked up, but he wasn't laughing, he was crying, and smiling at the same time.

"I remember that last run," he said, and wiped at his tears. "I looked back at Isaac just as we launched and he was high on the joy of it." He moved to sit on the floor opposite me. "The bridge's wood was rotten, it shifted, the car lost trajectory, Micah. You couldn't control the spin, we were in fate's hands."

Sometimes I dreamed about the instant it all went wrong, and in a few of those dreams I managed to handle the bucking trajectory of the car and land it safely. When I woke up from the dreams where no one died, I cried with the relief of it, until I realized it was just a delusion.

At that moment I didn't know what to say.

Chris still had tears in his eyes. I wish I could've cried, but I was empty inside.

"I hated you for a long time, blamed you for it all, my career chances gone, the fact that I'd lost my leg, but you know something? The accident wasn't your fault, we all wanted to be in that car, and when we crashed you dragged Isaac out and then you risked your own life in the fire to save me. You pulled me from the fire when I could have been burned alive, and you gave me a second chance at life."

"We shouldn't have been in the car," I said, willing Chris to admit that this all stemmed back to me borrowing the car. *Stealing the car.*

"But we were, and we were kids. I could have been driving if I hadn't had that beer. It was me who wanted to drive Daniel's car. I was so jealous he had the Chevy, and all I wanted to do was jump the bridge. You weren't supposed to be driving. If I'd crashed the car I'm not sure I would have been as brave as you to go back into the flames." He leaned toward me and reached for my arm, pushing back the shirt sleeves and exposing the twisted knot of scarring there. I let him touch me, he'd earned the right to see the evidence of my foolhardiness.

"You would have gone in," I defended, "Any one of us would have gone back in if they thought they could save the other."

He slid his hand down and laced our fingers, which felt wrong, but I didn't tug my hand away. If he wanted to hold my hand then I wasn't going to argue.

"I missed you," he said and bumped shoulders with me. "Isaac was dead, you were gone, and I was alone. We'd been three best friends for so long and then suddenly it was just me, and I wanted to die, and for a long time, yeah, I hated what you'd done. Then, I met Bonnie."

"A girlfriend?"

"No, she was far too good for me," he said with a smile. "She was in the next room to me, our age, leukemia, a beautiful girl who saw right through the absolute conviction I had that I wanted to die and called me on it."

He tipped his head back against the cabinet. "See, she *was* dying, and she didn't have a second chance. I could say that somehow I had an epiphany when she died, but it didn't happen then." He paused and I glanced at him and then back at our joined hands. "It happened the day I moved into my room at college. I didn't even want to apply, hell I'd barely scraped by at school, but y'know, special dispensation for the broken kid and all that." Then he laughed, as if that was so damn funny. "Daniel and Scott helped me fill out applications, to places I could still play ball, there were leagues out there for amputees, there was support, and hope. Then I didn't have room inside me to hate you anymore. I thanked you every time I went to sleep for getting me out of the burning car and allowing me to have the rest of my life."

Tears pricked at my eyes, I wasn't sure if they were tears of guilt, or shame, or pity. All I knew was that I was holding my best friend's hand and somehow, in the craziness of everything, he didn't hate me.

"I tried to find you then, as much as things like Google could help me, and your sister, I even asked Amy and Jeff where you were, but they said they didn't know. I know you sent them money, Jeff was real open about where he thought you made money, but they refused to let me have an address or anything. Christ knows who they thought they were punishing for what."

"I told them not to share where I was. I'm surprised they didn't tell you, would be one way to rid the family of the stain of murder."

I was half teasing, but it came out all wrong. I waited for Chris to go all disappointed on me, but he didn't, he simply looked at me and raised an eyebrow, and I felt shame again.

"I carried on trying to find you, Google failed me, and you and your sister had both vanished. I kept searching though, found you finally, working a horse training and education program at a ranch, but the next day I looked again and they'd taken the page featuring you down."

That was pretty easy to explain. The day I'd found my details on the K website I was furious. I didn't want anyone to know where I was. The only person who had my number was Rachel, and only because I'd tracked her down at college the day I'd left prison, leaving the message on her cell phone. She hadn't returned the call, or picked up, but I carried that old Nokia with the same number everywhere, just in case. I was her big brother, and I wanted her to know I was there for her if she needed me.

Chris interrupted my memories with a nudge. "I'd written the name of the ranch down though, and I wrote you a long letter."

"You did? Shit, I never received it."

"I wrote a letter, I didn't say I sent it." Chris chuckled, and leaned into me again, before untangling his fingers, and nimbly standing, using the counter for balance. He nodded to his coffee. "Bring that in, will you?"

I scrambled to stand, a lot less gracefully than Chris had. "Wait! Why didn't you send it?"

He went into the front room and I followed, both of us taking chairs, the coffees on the table between us.

"When I first got out of the hospital I wrote this protracted essay about how I was trying to forgive you. It was a self-righteous, holier-than-thou letter, but don't judge me, I was twenty-one and I was writing what I needed to let the poison out. I never sent that one either. But, this new letter, it was different because I knew in my heart there was never any blame on a single one of us. Not me for getting up in your face about your relationship with Daniel, forcing you to prove yourself by taking his keys. Or for drinking all that beer, or for Isaac encouraging us up to the bridge after I mentioned it. We were kids, Micah. Just kids."

Some nameless knot inside me loosened at his words. I knew Chris, and I believed what he was saying.

We talked for a while, the words stilted at times. We'd been best friends since we'd known what a friend was, but we were adults now, both nearing thirty, and a lot of time had passed.

"Now you're here are you getting back with Daniel?" Chris asked as I was getting my coat on to leave. That question blindsided me.

"No, I'm not staying in town long."

"Shame," he said.

"I'm not sure he's that happy I'm here after what I promised."

"He came back a few months back, bought the Henderson place."

"The Haunted House?"

"The same. Anyway, give him some space and he'll be back to macking on you as he used to."

The sense memory of our kiss pricked at me. "Not a chance of that happening," I said and tapped my lip where it was scabbing and healing.

"To be honest, Daniel could use a distraction in his life right now."

When I left it was nearly midnight, and the snow was heavy on the ground and in the air. Chris hugged me and I hugged him back. The guilt remained toxic in my soul, but his words were fighting for space and I wondered if one day I would have the kind of peace he had managed to find.

The beer was enough to take the edge off of the confrontation with my dad.

I'd gone to my usual hiding place; the Sheridan house. Only they were all out, except for Daniel, and wasn't that a bastard of a thing.

"You're home." I said when I stumbled into their kitchen, beer in hand.

"Wow, you're observant," Daniel commented and went back to reading whatever huge book it was that held his fascination. The kitchen table was covered in notebooks, and a pack of markers, and all I could think was that Daniel was so fucking gorgeous.

Sexy. Intriguing. And everything I'd ever wanted.

Which is why I was now tongue-tied, obviously.

"Yeah, so…how's college?"

Daniel glanced up at me over his reading glasses, and I couldn't help but think he was judging my lack of interesting conversation.

"Last year was good," he said, and took off his glasses, "One more year and I'm done with undergrad."

"And then what?" I knew Daniel had his whole life planned. He'd chosen his college for undergrad, moving into medical college, and then wanted to do residency at a hospital a long way from here. Or at least, that was what Chris had told me.

"Medical college, residency, home." The list was always the same, at the end of it all, Daniel was coming home to Whisper Creek to work in the family clinic with his dad, taking over the practice so he could retire one day.

"Cool."

I backed out of the kitchen, to leave, and next thing I knew he was following me out of the house, locking the door behind him.

"I need some air," he announced, and somehow, we fell into walking side by side. We ended up at the Henderson place, the Haunted House, and by unspoken agreement we went into the tangled mess of a garden, through the same gap in the fence, and unerringly to the

tree in the middle, surrounded by the mess of weeds and bushes.

There was no talking, but when he pulled me close and edged me back to the tree, and kissed me, it rocked my world.

Kissing Daniel was as inevitable as a sunrise, and as dramatic. I kissed with every part of me, was hard, and needed something. We got off there, right against the tree, me coming in my freaking pants, and Daniel? He held his cock and closed my hand over his, and I felt the pulse as he came.

And it was so right.

I DROVE past the Henderson place, with its ghostly appearance and its tangled undergrowth, on the way back to the ranch.

Why had Daniel bought the house? Was it recognition of what the place had meant to us as kids, or was it about the garden, or did he do it as a *fuck you* to what had happened there?

Who the hell knew?

16

DANIEL

CHRIS WALKED INTO MY HOUSE WITHOUT KNOCKING. THE entire family had keys, but the least they could do was knock.

"Let yourself in why, don't you. What if I had company?" I snapped at my brother as he made himself comfortable on my only kitchen chair.

"Whatever. Look, I spoke to Micah last night," Chris announced. I was already running close to being late for the clinic, but this was enough to stop me in my tracks. Why would Chris talk to Micah? What could they possibly have to say to each other?

"Yeah?" I tried for non-interested and Chris huffed at me

"He was my best friend growing up, Daniel. He came to see *me*, something about a favor for Rachel. I didn't give him a chance and I put a few things straight. Like how I don't blame him, and how me, him and Isaac were kids, and that I'm happy."

I couldn't believe what I was hearing, and a familiar

sadness gripped me. What was it with people going around and accepting things and offering forgiveness for past crimes? The weight on my chest was intense, my breathing restricted, and I could see myself giving into an abrupt panic attack. I'd kissed him, had feelings for him, and all this time he'd been planning to go behind my back and talk to Chris?

"Fuck's sake," I said, as I caught my breath. "Why would you even talk to him, Chris—?"

"Don't," Chris placed the flat of his hand on my chest. "Breathe."

I tried to breathe, but all I could see in my mind was Chris in the hospital, crying when he woke up.

Chris trying to take his own life.

"You need to talk to him," my brother murmured, and didn't move his hand. "I think you're confusing what happened to you in the emergency room situation, to the accident nine years ago. You need to forgive Micah, and yourself, and get your head straight."

"Don't talk crap," I snapped.

"You loved him."

"I was twenty-two, I didn't know what love was. It was two guys getting off." I was being crude, probably in the hope of getting Chris to back off, but he didn't stop. At least my breathing was evening out.

"Doesn't matter how old you were, you have to deal with what happened."

"I did. I do."

"No, you didn't."

I shoved at Chris to push him away, catching him in case he fell even as I did so. He shook off my help.

"You can push all you want, and I don't need you to

stop me falling anymore, big brother. Get your head out of your ass and talk to someone."

"I see a fucking shrink."

"I meant your family. You've been avoiding talking to me since you came home. Talk to us."

"Like you did?" I snapped, and he shook his head at my anger.

"I talked to you all. I trusted my family."

"You tried to fucking kill yourself."

That was the last, most awful thing I could say to my brother, and it hurt when I said it, but it was part of that poison inside me. I wanted him to be angry with me, I craved a confrontation so I could bury real emotions in anger.

"Nice," Sarcasm laced Chris' tone. "Is that all you've got?"

I urgently wanted him to lash out at me the same way I'd done at Micah at Isaac's grave, to free his aggression and anger at what I'd said. He just stood there and shook his head, smiling sadly, as if he had no anger inside him at all.

"Shit," I muttered. Every particle of adrenaline leaving me in a rush.

"Yep, you are."

"Chris—"

"You went back to college, you had a career, you left, and you avoided talking about the accident every single day I saw you. Now you're back and you still can't bear to look at me. Is it the scars? Or the fact I lost my leg? Do I make you feel sick to look at?"

"What? No!" I said, in shock.

"Then talk to us, talk to me, and for fuck's sake, stop

worrying about shit that happened nine years ago, and deal with the real issue from the hospital incident."

And then he left. I watched him get in his car from my front door and waited for some kind of understanding of what the hell had just happened.

I *had* talked to someone, after the hospital situation, the same woman who'd told me I had classic signs of PTSD and that I needed to be aware. The whole setup had been offered by the hospital as part of their insurance, and I went to a few sessions. The mandatory ones, at least. I hadn't needed an expert to tell me that I was in shock, nor that I held grief and horror at what had happened. People just needed to leave me alone and I would get over it, or at least hide it all away where it didn't matter so much.

Starting up here in Whisper Ridge, with a new counselor, with Devin, someone who knew the town and the families had been a very different kind of counseling, but it was working.

The waters were muddied. Was I ever going to get over these feelings of helplessness and fear, and was Chris right? Had I ever got to the point where I'd come to terms with his injury? Had I forgotten that in my run from the PTSD?

A text from Scott interrupted my thoughts. He said he wanted me to visit him at home that evening to talk about the deal to buy Lennox land.

I couldn't exactly say no as I, along with the rest of the Sheridan siblings, had invested in Sheridan Properties five years ago. It was our expression of faith in Scott, and his skill in being able to sell anything to anyone, and the fact he was hands-on with the projects. His mantra was that if it could be built then he wanted to know how. The company was a success, the investment solid, and he had a team working on my property.

As soon as work was done I headed for Scott's place, but I almost turned and left as soon as I saw Mom peering out from behind the drapes. I had nothing to worry about, they were overreacting and needed to leave me alone. Now was my chance to tell them that, and maybe I could convince Chris I wasn't a complete asshole.

"Took you guys long enough," I said when I walked in the door. They were all there, and I bet if they'd tried they could've gotten Mark, away at college, in on this over FaceTime.

Scott handed me a coffee. That was one thing I suppose; at least I got a hot mug to hide behind. I sat on the nearest chair and waited, assessing the emotions of the people ranged around me. Michelle was restless, walking the short distance between the sofa and the patio doors to the yard, rubbing her lower back. I narrowed my eyes as I watched her. The baby had definitely dropped. She wanted a home birth and the midwife was on alert, as was I.

The part of me that believed childbirth was a natural peaceful thing that would be less stressful at home warred with the doctor who had seen way too much to want Michelle this far away from the nearest hospital.

"Are you okay?" I asked her, and she nodded.

"I'm good, Junior is restless is all."

"I'm surprised they made you come," I said, and ignored the rest of my family just to focus on her.

"Wouldn't miss it for the world, big brother," she said, and smiled at me softly.

Dad cleared his throat, evidently, he was family spokesperson.

"We're worried about you, son," he began.

I sighed heavily.

I gave my standard answer. "You don't need to be. I'm okay. I'm happy in Whisper Ridge, and yes I moved here a year earlier than the grand plan, but that is okay." I realized I was using the word okay, and that wasn't going to convince anyone. 'Okay' was one of those words like 'fine' which meant nothing at all.

Chris and Michelle exchanged looks, and it irritated me that they didn't know where to start to talk to me.

"You don't tell us anything about what happened in Charlotte," Michelle finally said. Chris nodded.

"You saw the news," I offered.

"Maybe it's time to tell us your version," Mom prompted. "Just so we can get an idea of—"

"Of what, Mom?"

"Of how you're feeling, maybe?" This was from Michelle, who had taken a seat directly opposite me.

"What exactly do you want to know? Huh?"

"How about everything, moron?" Scott said, and my control snapped.

"You want to know how many bullets were embedded in the wall? Or the fact the blood wouldn't wash away from the shattered tiles? Or how I held my colleague even after she was dead?" I was staying calm as I asked the questions, but I could feel I was beginning to let my emotions get the better of me.

"Daniel!" Dad warned, and I suppose I should have felt remorseful, but I barreled ahead.

"Okay then here goes. The guy with the gun, he was known to us, we'd treated his brother the week before, not me, it was this other doc, Julia—we call her Jules." I probably needed to correct that to the sentence 'we used to call her Jules', because she was dead now. I didn't need to though, everyone in this room knew that Julia Maine had died. That much had been in the news reports, along with a picture of her, and her husband and new baby daughter.

"Go on," Chris encouraged. I hadn't even realized I'd stopped talking as I remembered that photo. Julia had only been back to work a week, and she'd been killed, by a man who had engineered his way through security using friendship and guile.

"Emmet Hutton had come into the emergency room with his brother. Julia managed to save the brother, and he was discharged. Emmet came back, a week later, with flowers and chocolate. They let him in…" I stopped to get my thoughts straight. "His brother was dead, killed that day in a gang related drive-by. Emmet had this thing in his head that it was our fault for releasing his brother early, and he wouldn't listen to any of us. Held a gun on me for the longest time, and then at Jules' head and shot her. Right in front of me."

I glanced around at the faces before me. I knew each one so well, and I could see their reactions, read the small tics. Scott frowned, he hated not having control in a situation. Michelle wouldn't look directly at me. Chris was holding her hand. He did that a lot, touching people, something he'd done since his stay at the hospital, a kind of reassurance that he was present in the room I guess.

"The security team said we should wait for a negotiator, but I had other ideas. I mean, I've had training, and I thought I could get through to him. I tried to talk him down, explained how someone else dying wouldn't fix the loss of his brother. He was growing more agitated as each second passed, and I kept trying to talk him down. I wasn't the target though, he was looking for, Julia was, and he called her forward. I stopped her, pushed her behind me, but she wouldn't stay. If she'd stayed then maybe the bullet would have hit me and she would still be with her baby."

I closed my eyes briefly. "Emmet didn't wait to talk to her, or negotiate, he wanted to kill her, and he shot her in the face. I caught her as she fell." I brushed the front of my shirt. "The blood was everywhere on me, the floor, and I held her in my hands as he turned the gun on himself right in front of me."

"Holy shit," Scott said.

"The cops told me it wouldn't have mattered even if we had waited. Emmet was icily determined, left notes and a letter at home. He'd planned everything out, befriended the staff, thanked them for caring for his brother." I stopped and breathed through the pain in my chest.

"Jesus," Chris murmured.

"But it is my fault. I see us standing there with a gun on us and I am so confident, so fucking arrogant, thinking I know what's for the best, and I talked to the guy, and he shot her. So, it doesn't matter what the cops say, it could have ended differently."

A chorus of noise was muddled in my head as everyone tried to talk over each other. Finally, the loudest voice won. The same one that always made us listen. Mom.

"Everyone, stop!" she shouted, and to everyone's credit they all ceased their vocal support of whatever I had done.

They didn't know enough to tell me it wasn't my fault.

I remembered every second of it and could replay it in my head in slow motion. I could walk a person through every word, every movement, every error, and at the end of it all it was me, Doctor *freaking* Sheridan who had fucked up. Of course, my counselor in the city told me that blame wasn't a good thing. But it was going to Devin and talking to him that tipped me over the edge, He'd connected how I was reacting to what happened that day to misplaced guilt for what had happened nine years ago, I called bullshit on that but the thought that maybe he was right was there in my head, niggling and poking at me.

"Is this what you feel you have to live with?" Mom asked, oh so very gently. She was probably frightened I might snap if she asked the wrong question, and yeah, I was miserable and jumpy, but I wasn't on the edge of losing control. Not with my family.

Well, not in the front room of Scott's house, anyway.

"It's not that I choose to live with it, I just do, Mom."

She nodded. "I understand that, sweetheart."

My mom and dad had taught me and my siblings that a person could take on the world and win, that if they tried hard enough they could have everything. They didn't raise quitters, and it was only that which kept me going some days. Otherwise I think I would have been consumed with guilt. As it was, according to my counselor, I had parceled up guilt from the car accident when I was younger, added it to the feelings about Julia being shot, then put it to one side and the whole mess was manifesting into post-traumatic stress.

"Survivor's guilt," Michelle said, and sat next to me, grasping my hand. "We read all about it."

Of course, they had. Likely it was Dad who found

articles or books, and spent days making notes to discuss with the rest of the family, same as he had done when we'd brought Chris home from the hospital after the accident.

"An educated person is a strong person," he said to us then, and he was no doubt saying it to my mom and siblings now.

"Please don't worry about me."

I might as well have been speaking to a room full of empty chairs for all the notice my family would take of that plea. I would still get food baskets from Mom, coffee at work from Dad, and visits and texts from the rest of them.

"So, can we talk about the Micah thing?" Chris asked, and stared right at me.

I could have said something along the lines of "what about the Micah thing?" but there was really no point. "You mean about me hitting him? Or are we looking way back to the accident, or even further to me and him being together?"

"It's all of it, sweetheart, punching someone isn't like you," Mom said, and looked stricken. If there was one person in this family I hated upsetting, it was her. She had this way of appearing so sad and I felt responsible for breaking her heart.

"Unresolved anger," I summarized, "No connection to the shooting. Micah promised he wouldn't come back, add in everything else and I just took one look at his face, and hit him."

"I've seen his face," Michelle began. "It wasn't just one punch."

I shook my head. "No, it was only one but I caught him by surprise. Also, a few days back he kissed me."

Silence. So quiet I could hear my breathing. Why the hell had I told them that?

"With tongues?" Scott asked, and I didn't care if he was trying to lighten the mood, that was an asshole thing to ask.

"Fuck you," I snapped.

"Boys!" Mom intervened.

"Did you kiss him back?" Scott persisted.

"That's none of your fu—freaking business."

Scott and Chris exchanged knowing glances and I knew what one of them was going to say next, and I wanted desperately for them to not go there. But then, what kind of intervention would it have been if they didn't call me on everything that might be giving me grief.

"Is there something more to this with Micah? Do you still have feelings for him?" Chris asked, after he'd clearly drawn the short straw in the "asking Daniel the hard question stakes".

"Jesus, Chris, it was one kiss." I hadn't expected him to cut to the chase quite so quickly.

Chris sighed dramatically. "One kiss is all it takes," he pointed out.

Scott couldn't meet my gaze, but his lips were pressed together tightly, holding something back. I didn't give him a chance to let it all out and I forged ahead.

"Seeing him again now, has dug up memories I don't want to think about. Not good ones for sure, and added to what I'm dealing with, it's hard. Is that all you wanted to ask?"

Again, there was a silence and I almost left then, thinking we were done.

"Are you seeing someone? A counselor?" Dad asked,

ever the practical one, and expert at guiding family discussions.

"Devin Hastings," I admitted. "Over in Collier Springs." Devin was someone I'd known in school and I was talking to him on a regular basis. He was a good listener and was helping me to work my way through what had happened in Charlotte. He'd only recently moved back to Whisper Ridge. I think he'd burned out the same as I had in the city, but for someone who listened to people as much as he did, he wasn't a man to share his own issues with anyone else.

"So, we're done, right?" I stood, and made a show of stretching, and then went to the door. "Thank you for caring, guys, it means a lot," I said, and left.

As I walked through the snow back to my house I felt a flash of anger at Chris' question, but I quickly pushed it down. It was no one's business if I had feelings, or if Micah had kissed me.

Nor that I wanted to kiss him back but didn't.

And no, I had absolutely no deep dark feelings for the man who had stolen my brother's life and killed another. Well, except for the obvious anger. Right?

Liar.

17

MICAH

Chris' words about all three of us in the car accident sharing responsibility haunted me every waking hour for the next few days, in rotation with the memories of the kiss I'd pressed to Daniel's lips.

The fact he felt there was shared blame didn't sit with me very well. Yes, Isaac had been drinking and so had Chris. But it was me who had stolen the keys. Even if Chris wanted to take some responsibility for spurring me on, I wasn't ready for him to take it.

Back on the day of the accident, I'd reacted to Chris's teasing, telling me that I was spending too much time mooning over Daniel, that I was losing my spark, that I was boring when I refused to do anything fun now I had a boyfriend.

God, I'd lost it. I was nineteen, and my entire being revolved around being a man, a rebel, the one who headed for trouble and then danced away at the last moment to avoid punishment. I'd had no chance to go to college, my life was mapped out for me on the ranch. But I loved it, and I didn't care, and hell, it had burned Dad when I'd used the money he gave me for college to pay for Rachel. God, he'd hated that. He'd already lost his cool with me coming out as gay, but then to go right on into a relationship with Daniel? Shit, the teasing I got, all the constant gay jokes, they somehow became tiny little slivers of glass that worked their way under my skin.

I left Daniel's bed that night and took the keys. Used Daniel's car.

That was on me.

And the worst of it, in those quiet times when I couldn't think of anything else, all I could recall was the kiss. So, I did what I was best at. I ignored my feelings. Hid them all away and let them fester, and concentrated hard on the ranch.

I slipped into a routine. One that I needed. Waking early, working with the horses, braving the cold, lugging hay. It was good, honest, physical work, and it centered me more than confronting any memories did.

The guys I'd hired worked hard, and slowly but surely, I began to pull together the image from my childhood memories of the ranch.

I'd deliberately hired out of Collier Springs, but it hadn't taken long for one of them to find out who I was, and the gossip that followed me. Two days actually before they began to side-eye me, and I didn't have time for it so I ignored it.

And I would keep ignoring it until they refused to work for me.

Individually, they groused at me that I should wait for spring, but I wasn't sure how long it would be before the compound, or the cops, caught up with me — I needed things done, to make the ranch safe at least. Three weeks had passed since we'd arrived, but it seemed like yesterday, for the most part.

If it wasn't for how Laurie had changed, I wouldn't even have thought we'd been there that long. He'd taken to following me around, still not saying much, aside from please and thank you, but he listened to any instructions I gave, and had taken a shine to me.

I guess I *was* his uncle after all.

We'd built a snowman after morning chores, and even though it was lopsided Laurie had taken the whole design very seriously. Now we'd moved onto tidying up in the barn, pulling together old ropes and chains and sorting through them.

"Hold this tight," I said, and handed the rope to Laurie, waiting for him to grip it hard enough, then easing back on my hold. The little guy was small, but he'd filled out a bit since we'd arrived. The "place", as Rachel, him and me had taken to calling the compound, hadn't believed in food as being necessary. Prayer had nearly killed the kid and real food was making its mark. Everything had to be introduced slowly. He'd never had chocolate cake. One slice and he'd vomited everywhere, crying that it was so good and all he'd wanted.

Rachel had given him a mouthful the next night and stopped it there. A few days later, two. Funny how introducing him slowly to something that was probably bad for him, was counted as such a success. I couldn't imagine what he'd gone through and I think I watched him too much, waiting for the cracks to show.

Maybe at five his resilience was higher, hell, maybe he'd forget some of the things he'd seen. Rachel said that she wanted him to see someone, I just said she should include herself in that as well. That was the end of that conversation. I did do some research at the library in Collier Springs, and printed the whole lot out, leaving it on her bed. There were names on there of reputable counselors who specialized in kids.

But Laurie was doing okay, right? He was working with me, and we should have probably registered him to start school after Christmas. Although that was a problem. The whole Laurie issue was a problem. He'd seen everything and how the hell did we stop him from telling people?

"Look Uncle Micah, this is what I saw."

I had my smile ready and turned back from where the other end of the rope was coiled over a post, to see what he'd achieved now.

I froze, horrified. Carefully I moved closer, holding out a hand, and talking really quietly.

"What are you doing, buddy?" I reached him before he could do himself an injury. He'd wrapped the rope around his neck, and his face was twisted in a grimace, his tongue poking out, as if he'd been hanged.

This is what I saw? What did he mean?

I unwrapped the rope and removed it. Picked him up and held him close. Then I carried him all the way back to the house, went straight into Rachel's room and held him tight as I shook her awake. She rolled over in her sleep, looking pale, bags under her eyes, and pain carved into her face. She'd had a migraine yesterday, and she was puffy and listless. I didn't think that was normal, but she seemed too tired to even care.

What the hell was I trying to achieve? How did I think

that hiding out here was a good thing? Rachel needed proper health care, Laurie needed to talk to someone.

I took the bull by the horns. "Get dressed, Rachel. Laurie and I will be outside."

Rachel balked when we got to the car. She'd mostly gone along with me encouraging her to get dressed, and put her coat and shoes on, but when faced with the car she came to a dead stop.

"Micah?" She asked, and her single word held a hundred questions. I wish I had answers, but I didn't.

Instead I hugged her and Laurie and just whispered two words. *Trust me.*

Making it off the ranch on the unplowed roads wasn't simple, but as soon as we were on the main road it was way too easy to get into Whisper Ridge itself. There was very little thinking time and before I knew it we were parked outside the back of the Whisper Ridge Diner. I turned in my seat and Rachel stared back at me massaging her temples with her fingers.

"You need to see the midwife," I said.

"It's just a headache," she defended. "I've been pregnant before, had Laurie without this fuss, I don't need someone poking at me."

"Humor me." I glanced back at Laurie who was staring out of the window with wide eyes. "Come on, Laurie, let's get your mommy taken care of and find cake."

I've never seen a kid move so fast, clambering from the back seat and following me out of the car, holding up his arms. I could handle carrying my nephew. He needed it, and hell, I needed it too.

The three of us walked the short distance from diner to the clinic. Rachel was dragging behind. I slowed and offered her my free arm, and she clung to it. The sidewalk was clear but she was holding onto me as if she was going to fall over. I went into protective mode, waiting to help her into the clinic's reception. She stood just inside, tugging at her long skirt, and I should have realized something when everyone turned to stare at the new people stepping inside.

Everyone stared. No one said a thing but their expressions said it all. Did they know who I was? Or was it the fact that Rachel was pale, pregnant, and close to falling over in her huge puffy coat? I crossed quickly to reception and to a woman I couldn't fail to recognize. Chloe, Sheriff Windham's wife, not looking a day older than the last time I'd seen her.

"My sister needs to see the midwife."

Chloe shook her head, "I'm sorry Micah. She's only here two days a week. We share her with two other clinics. Can the doctor help?"

What did I know about who helped a pregnant woman, surely it was a midwife, what could a doctor do? Daniel was adamant she had to see a midwife. I glanced back at Rachel who had taken an end seat, still in her coat, and Laurie standing between her legs.

"I don't know," I admitted and waited for Chloe to tell me what a stupid man I was, and why wasn't I looking out for my sister. Chloe glanced past me at Rachel and pursed her lips.

Here it comes.

"I think Doctor Sheridan would be the place to start, I'll book her in with some details. Can you help me with that?" She forged ahead without me saying I could help, and passed me forms to fill in. I answered what I could:

name, address, and birthdate. That was as far as the questions went, so I guess requests about Laurie and her pregnancy were confidential. Not that the people in the room hadn't made judgements by now.

I wasn't worried by that.

"I also need to register my nephew."

I took the seat next to Rachel and made the time to scan the room. I recognized a couple of people, one girl I'd been at school with. I remember she'd been one of the better ones at school. I think one of the guys sitting with stitches in his forehead had been a few years above me. They regarded me with curiosity, and I returned their curious stares with a nod.

I was out of my depth sitting there, I didn't know what to do about Rachel, but the worst issue was Laurie. What did I do? Who did I talk to? He needed a check-up at least, and help in so many other ways. More than half of me hoped it was Doctor Sheridan senior who was seeing the family, but we probably weren't going to be so lucky.

"Rachel Lennox, the doctor will see you now, room two," Chloe said.

I helped Rachel to stand, and she didn't let go of me.

"We're not separating," she said, low and close to my ear. "Stay with me."

I hefted Laurie a little and he wrapped his arms around my neck. "Okay."

"Don't let them stop you."

"I won't, I promise."

I opened the door to the doctor's rooms and a flood of memories hit me, of visits as a kid, the time I'd broken my arm in third grade and Dad had thought I was making it up. Doctor Sheridan senior had soon put him right. Or the time I'd had bronchitis, and Mom had brought me to see the doctor. I remember his room was a chaos of photos and pictures on the wall, and his desk had been covered in leather bound books. But it wasn't his old room we were being taken to, room two hadn't even existed before. I recall it was some kind of meeting room back when I used to visit, but clearly now room had been made for the new Doctor Sheridan.

I let Rachel go in first, and followed her, closing the door behind me and waiting awkwardly.

Daniel was there, the picture of professionalism, gorgeous and unruffled in a suit and tie, in a room that was perfectly tidy and organized. There were photos and pictures, but they were in a pile to one side, and instead of leather books there was a computer on the desk. He came forward and shook Rachel's hand. I looked back at him and he arched an eyebrow, fully aware that I had been checking out his office. I lowered my gaze in case he saw any of my reaction to seeing him standing there. I could see him clearly in a suit at my mom's funeral.

I wondered if he'd gone to my dad's funeral. I wondered if anyone had gone. That lonely, broken old man hadn't had many friends left. Not after his wife had died, and he'd cut himself off, and then following that what had happened to me and what I'd done.

"Glad you could come down to see us. I put a call in with Melanie, our midwife, she was planning on visiting in the morning, but she's heading over here now as a favor to me."

Yeah, that sounded right. Daniel, the man who could make things happen at the snap of a finger.

Then he was talking, "You can go back outside if you

like." I realized he was talking to me at the same time as Rachel moved closer and held my arm.

"I want him to stay."

Daniel didn't argue. He simply pulled out another chair from the side and gestured for me to sit. I wasn't the father, but I guessed Rachel could have who the hell she wanted in the room with her.

"Hello Laurie," he said. Laurie stared at him as if he'd been offered a handful of spiders. I suppose that was another thing he hadn't learned, the concept of random friendliness from total strangers. I shifted Laurie to my left arm and shook.

"Micah," he said, and held my hand a little longer than was absolutely necessary. In the end it was me who shook the hold free, and went back to hugging Laurie close before sitting on the chair in the corner by the desk.

"Rachel's having migraines," I explained, "And I looked it up, and I'm worried."

Daniel nodded, then turned his back to me and Laurie, "Could I ask you—?"

She thrust out the small sample in the plastic container he'd given her at the ranch, and he smiled at her. Then gestured for her to go behind the curtain. She hesitated at first and looked at me.

"Not going anywhere," I said.

What evil had my sister seen to make her so desperate and scared?

The knock on the door was the precursor to Melanie-the-midwife coming in, and then she kind of took over in a flurry of motion and encouragement. She even managed to get Rachel to the medical room for a proper examination.

Which left me and Laurie with Daniel.

“I’d like you to look at Laurie,” I said, before he had the chance to kick me out of the office. I knew damn well there were no more people in the waiting room. We’d been the last in, and he couldn’t throw us out. I was going to fight my corner for Laurie, whatever our pasts.

“Of course,” he said, which threw me for a loop. I realized I had gone on the defensive and Laurie whimpered in my arms from where I’d been holding him way too tight.

Daniel came out from behind his desk and crouched by me. So close, that I could see his dark eyes. Some people might have thought they were just brown, the same as his hair, but when I was that close I could can see tiny flecks of amber around the pupils. And his hair wasn’t just brown, in some light it had a hint of red in it. He still wore it in the same style, long on top, short on the sides, and I knew that if I touched it, it would be soft. He used to spend ages on his hair, and I’d watched him from his bed on more than one occasion. As the oldest Sheridan child, he’d had the room over the garage, and it had made me staying over easy. At nineteen I was sleeping with a hot twenty-two-year-old, and I was in love.

“Earth to Micah,” Daniel waved in front of my face, and I snapped back to the present. “I said, could you encourage Laurie onto the scales for me?”

I did what he said, balanced Laurie there, and pried his fingers from around my neck, until he stood unaided, looking at his feet and ignoring all of Daniel’s questions. When Daniel went to lift his shirt, his stethoscope in his ears, ready to listen to Laurie’s chest, the kid freaked out. I picked him up to soothe him and waited for Daniel to get angry.

He didn't show any sign of anger. "Sit down guys," he said, and this time I took the chair opposite him, and waited for him to go back behind his desk, but he didn't do that, he crouched by us again. "I am bound by doctor patient confidentiality," he began. He wasn't talking to Laurie, of course. He was talking right to me. "I need to know what is going on here."

"He has to talk to someone," I blurted out. "So does Rachel."

"Can you tell me why, Micah?"

This wasn't the man who'd punched me into a gravestone, this was Doctor Daniel Sheridan, and I could trust this incarnation of him. But if I told *him*, knowing how friendly he was with the sheriff, and if Rachel and Laurie talked about the compound, then I wouldn't have time to settle them and move on. I needed the cops to follow me, I had to leave a trail they could find, so they left Rachel and Laurie behind.

There were still no news reports. Was it possible that the compound was so off the grid that a murder would never be reported? Was Rachel right about them?

"Can you recommend someone?" I asked.

"I can, hang on." He reached for the phone on the desk, a shiny iPhone in a purple case, and scrolled through his contacts. Then he stood from his crouch and stretched his legs. He handed me a piece of paper with a scribbled name and number, Devin Hastings. "Devin is a counselor at a practice, and he also has partners who specialize in minors," he said. I began to leave and find Rachel but Daniel stopped me with a hand on my arm. "You can't keep everything secret," he said. "Not where children are involved. Laurie is vulnerable, remember that."

"You don't need to tell me, I know."

"If I can help at all..." He offered me a lifeline. Abruptly, I felt as if I could ask him to tell me what to do and it would solve everything. Then like ice water on my face I realized that this was something I had to do with Rachel and Laurie on our own.

"No, we're good," I said.

When I made it outside, with Rachel leaning on me and Laurie curled into my neck I had to wonder at Daniel's parting words about not keeping secrets.

Were they a gentle warning from someone I used to know? Or a threat from someone in a position of responsibility?

18

DANIEL

I waited only long enough to make sure that Micah and his family had gone, and then I left the clinic to find Neil. Being the sheriff, he would know what to do with the things I had seen that morning, but he wasn't at his desk. I wanted to talk informally, off the record, but I was thwarted. Apparently, he was out toward Collier Springs, and would be back in a while, and I was left with nothing to do but wait.

I managed to get hold of him by phone, and just hinted at issues that I had spotted with Rachel and her son. That I thought there was something else going on, or at least there had been in the past.

He rang me straight back, apologizing for missing the call, and he said he'd look into it, maybe have a chat with Rachel. What else could I do? I wasn't going to make things official, not right now.

Then I called Devin. He had appointments all day, or so his secretary said. I left a short message, then texted that I'd referred someone to him, without going into details. I wanted to tell him everything, that little Laurie Lennox was petrified and uncertain. He appeared to be viewing things, normal objects, for the first time, and that none of it felt right. I wanted to explicitly say there had been abuse, but I didn't know for sure, because Rachel hadn't said a damn thing. But I couldn't say any of that, not on an answering machine.

And what about Micah? I wanted to talk to *someone* about him, and the fact he was there, and that somehow, I was losing the battle to remain angry and resentful where he was concerned.

I guessed I could cover some of that when I saw Devin myself. I had my next appointment in a week and I had a mental list of everything I wanted to cover

Mom was home, one of her rare days when she wasn't at gardening club, or aqua aerobics, or working her part-time hours at the veterinary practice in town. She would be my voice of reason, I knew it.

"Daniel! Come in, I need your help." She disappeared into the house, and I followed. She pointed up at the tall cupboard in the corner. "Fetch me down the big plate at the back, would you?"

Mom, being a shade over five foot, was the smallest in our house. I pulled down the plate and smiled, it was the special cookie plate, which meant there were cookies lurking somewhere in the kitchen, although I was disappointed I couldn't smell them. That was something else my mom did well, made the most amazing baked goods. It was a wonder none of us had made it out of childhood with sugar addiction issues.

"Margie wants to borrow this," she said, and my eagerness for cookies was dealt a serious blow. I could've really done with coffee and cookies and a comforting hug from my mom.

How freaking stupid is that.

"Sit yourself down, sweetheart, coffee? I think I have some cake left if you're interested?"

"Always."

She busied herself around the large kitchen, the kind of room I aspired to having in my house, all big counters, loads of cupboard space, and a coffee maker that I envied. When I had coffee and a huge slice of carrot cake in front of me, as well as Fudge, the aged family cat, on my lap, she settled down and sighed.

"What's wrong?" she asked. Cutting straight to the chase was another of my mom's strong points. She wasn't one to sit and listen to great long introductions, she wanted to get to the crux of the matter immediately. Probably part and parcel of having five kids in eight years.

"You mean besides the whole fucked in the head jumping at shadows thing?"

She patted my hand. "I'll let you have that curse," she tutted. "But, there's something more."

"Micah came into the clinic today, with Rachel and his nephew, Laurie. The kid is cute, five, but something's wrong with him. Not medically, although despite weighing him, he wouldn't let me touch him at all. He's underweight for his age, but he seems well. I just don't know what to do."

Mom regarded me steadily and sipped her coffee. "About Laurie or his uncle?"

That was Mom, asking all the hard questions.

"I went to talk to Neil, but he's off-site until later. I'm worried about what happened to Laurie and Rachel, and why Micah brought them back to Whisper Ridge, why Rachel looks so broken, and why Laurie hides in his uncle's arms."

"Officially? Or as friends?"

That was another question I needed to answer for myself. Laurie was on edge, scared, wide-eyed, clinging to Micah, and had the classic signs of abuse. He was withdrawn, fearful, and I didn't get to check for bruises or other signs, but something wasn't right. I'd seen it before in hospitals, kids coming in, scared of their own shadows, and I had to listen to my gut. But then there was Rachel. I'd seen bruises on her, burns on her back, two scars across her belly that looked as if someone had taken a knife and cut her. She'd suffered abuse. Laurie had as well. Then there was Micah. He was protecting them, holding onto them, keeping them safe.

"Not officially," I finally said after thinking it through. "I just want to know what I'm dealing with. I gave Devin's number to Micah and all I can hope is that Micah takes Laurie to him."

"What is it you want the sheriff to find out for you?"

"Good question," I murmured, and pushed the plate toward her a little. She said that cake stolen from one of her kids had no calories, and it had become a game to see if you could keep Mom from taking some of the precious cake. Either that or we had to give in, which was the route I took. I cut her a bit and placed it on the side of the plate and she took it with a smile. "It's my duty to report it, as a doctor." That much was true. I should've been talking to Neil, and making a formal report, but what if I did that and whoever had hurt Laurie and Rachel was found, and I made it a million times worse.

Before Charlotte and what I'd seen in the emergency room, I would have followed the rules and reported my findings through appropriate channels, but I was a wiser, more experienced man.

Experienced in the hateful, evil, acts that one person can do to another.

"But you're not writing up a report, you're sitting here eating cake and talking to me. What is the real issue here, is it Micah himself?"

I turned my hands over to examine the knuckles. The marks on them had gone, as had most of the temper that had manifested itself in the need to try to mark Micah. What was left in its place was an unsettled emotion, of not quite knowing what to do with my feelings for Micah.

There was old anger, certainly, but he was so protective of his family.

The kitten was tiny, a little gray thing that Micah held in his hands at our back door.

"What's wrong?" Mom said, reaching for Micah, and the kitten. I hadn't seen his face, but when he stepped into the kitchen I saw one side of his face was scarlet and he was crying.

"D—D—Dad won't let m-me keep her," he hiccupped and I copied the noise and sniggered. I'm not sure he even heard me, but Mark did and my littlest brother thought I was super funny.

"Sit down, sweetheart." Mom bustled around finding cake and milk and a cardboard box. The cake was triple chocolate fudge and we weren't allowed any until after dinner, but Micah was?

How was that fair?

Mom went into the laundry and pulled out some sweatshirts, and I watched horrified as she placed them in the box and then took the kitten from Micah's hands. The kitten snuggled into the material.

"That's my Cubs jersey," I protested. Not that I wore it, the sleeves were too short, and it was tight, still, it was mine, and being the eldest of five meant my shit was always disappearing. One day Chris would play for the Cubs, we all knew it, and I wanted to keep all my shirts.

Freaking cat. Freaking Micah.

"Hush," Mom warned and I subsided. "You found it?" she asked Micah.

"Uh huh," he said and hiccupped another sob.

"What a baby," I whispered to Mark, who nodded as if I was making sense.

I looked up and Micah was staring at me, and he was crying, and I felt like a complete bastard for laughing at him right then.

We'd had the lecture, how Micah and Rachel had lost their mom, and how their dad was always sad. Our parents didn't need to tell us to be nice to them, I wasn't a bad person, but Micah was twelve and he was crying as Mark did.

The kitten was kind of cute, but I was more worried about what was happening to my jersey, and the chocolate cake, to spend any time fussing over it. Not that I could if I wanted to. Micah was in the way. Up close he had a cut on his face, and blood had dried there.

He'd probably fallen over. He was always doing that, explaining he'd walked into doors, and fallen down the stairs. Not that his place had stairs.

"What will happen to it?" He was fierce now, standing there guarding the kitten. It was kind of funny.

"Don't worry sweetheart, I'll take care of this. The kitten can come live here."

I immediately pushed past Micah and retrieved my jersey, the kitten rolling on its back and batting at me with tiny paws. No interloper was getting my stuff, and I was going to tell him.

Only he looked up at me, and he was crying, and he didn't care I'd taken the jersey. He just wanted help for the kitten, and I felt like crap for being so nasty.

I handed back the jersey, muttered a sorry, and left the kitchen.

I STROKED FUDGE'S FUR, she was elderly, and quieter now, but she loved nothing more than being petted and fussed over. The cat had been out in one of the Lennox Ranch barns.

"You remember the day Micah brought Fudge here? What was he, twelve, and bawling his eyes out?"

"Of course, I do. The kid never caught a break with his dad, he was always here up in Chris' room as soon as his chores were done at the ranch."

"I know, but do you recall specifically, that day, with the kitten."

Mom sipped her coffee. "Yes?"

"I teased him so bad about crying, sat right here doing homework and I laughed at him with Mark. I remember all Micah could say was that his dad had wanted to throw the kitten out, and Micah wanted it to have a family that cared. He held the cat so close, wouldn't let anyone else touch her, and you calmed Micah down. Fed him cake I think."

"My chocolate heaven cake, with the fudge frosting. We called the kitten Fudge because of the cake," Mom smiled fondly.

"You put the kitten in a box with my Cubs jersey and promised Fudge could stay here, and Micah was so happy that it would have a good home."

Mom frowned at me. "Where are you going with this?"

"I saw it in his eyes, Mom. Even though I was pissed at him, and that you were using my Cubs jersey, I saw right through him. Back then, there was desperation, a plea for help, and a fierce protectiveness. I saw the same thing again today, I'd forgotten that part of him."

Mom reached over and took my hand. "It's hard to memorize the good stuff when the bad things seem so big."

I stared into my coffee, a hundred thoughts swirling at once. I trusted my mom would have some advice for me, because that was who she was.

"He kissed you," she prompted gently. "Did you kiss him back? Did you want to?"

"I can't Mom, what he did to our family, to Chris, how can I justify what I think I might feel against all of that?"

"But you feel something?"

I looked into her dark eyes, and knew I had to be honest, if not to her then at least to myself. Seeing Micah again had knocked me off balance.

"I can just imagine being with Micah now, taking him to family gatherings. How do you think that would go?"

"You think we wouldn't want it?"

"You're really asking that? Chris wouldn't be able to handle having him there."

"Sweetheart, have you had an in-depth talk with your brother?"

"Which one?" I asked even though I could guess who she meant, it was always the same with my mom. Chris and I had been so close growing up, but we'd lost some of the connection. I'd solved it by staying away at college and then working in hospitals, but now I was back, and I really needed to connect on a personal level rather than sitting at opposite ends of the table at Sunday dinner.

"Chris?"

"You mean have I spoken to him apart from the intervention when he asked me if I have any feelings for Micah." I couldn't help the dry tone of my voice.

She squeezed my fingers. "It's all such a mess. But your brother is a good man, strong and determined, the same as you. I think maybe Chris would rather have the brother who is happy than the one who carries around the weight of so many decisions."

"I can't help it, I don't want to make the wrong decision."

"What's done is done." Mom carried on with all her innate motherly wisdom. "Chris has come to terms with everything, he accepts his own part in it, and sweetheart, he doesn't need you thinking you need to be at war with Micah over something that puts him in the middle."

I immediately felt contrite, and my natural reaction was to be defensive, but I knew better than to show that to my mom. She watched me closely as I processed in my head what she'd had to say. She was telling me to think things over, knowing that anything I did or said to Micah impacted Chris, but that I also needed to be my own man. And she was right as usual.

The same way she was right about talking seriously to Chris. Unless I really listened to Chris, not just grudgingly, about what had happened all those years ago, I would never be able to get over myself. As a doctor I was the first person to advocate talking issues out, expounding at length about the benefits of getting your emotions out to be examined closely.

I hugged Mom hard when I left. As her eldest son, I liked to think we had a special bond because of that. For a while I sat in the car and thought about what I'd just done.

Was it really true that "what's done is done"? Was Mom right?

The hospital was so quiet. We were taking it in turns sitting by Chris' bed, each dealing with his overdose in our own way. Michelle comforted, Scott confronted, Mark was quiet, and me? I was in shock. I knew clinically that it was shock. I felt sick, and shaky, and I couldn't think straight.

The paramedics had been quick, got Chris to Collier Springs Hospital, and there we all stayed waiting for Chris to wake up.

But right now, it was my turn, so it was me that Chris saw first. He blinked his eyes open, looking confused, and then he shouted.

Over and over.

"No. No. Micah! No!"

The nurses calmed him down.

When it was my turn to sit with him again, at some ungodly hour of the morning, holding his hand and wishing I could make it all better, he opened his eyes again. He focused on me.

"I hate him, Danny."

"Who?" I asked him, even though I knew.

"Micah. I hate Micah." Then he closed his eyes. "I want to die."

I HEADED STRAIGHT BACK for Neil, but was frustrated in my attempt to clear my head of everything I was thinking. He was still out on some kind of call at the Ridge, and my intention to talk about Micah and his small family, informally, to the local sheriff, was thwarted. I checked back in at the clinic, but there was nothing I needed to handle, so, at five p.m., in the dark and snow, I was off the clock.

The short hours were something else I found it hard to get used to. The hospital work had been frantic from beginning to end of shift, and shifts often blurred into one another. Sometimes at this clinic I felt bored, doodling ideas for outreach and support that I could package together to offer the people who were up in the mountains, or out by the lake in country isolation. At least I was putting my "bored time" to use. I walked home, sticking to the cleared sidewalk, and headed for the back of the house and the tangled garden. Something drew me there, away from the warmth of my home and into the expanse of trees and bushes that I was only just beginning to tame.

For the longest time I stared at the remains of the tree I'd destroyed and ended up kicking it with the toe of my shoe. If I believed in symbolism then the fact there were two tiny shoots on one side of it would mean something. Renewal. Forgiveness? Who the hell knew? Damn thing needed pulling out, roots and all.

I walked around the front, pulling out keys and not looking up as I should have been. Maybe then I would have had some warning.

"Daniel."

I came to a dead stop. Micah was on the broken porch, every inch the rough, sexy cowboy in a sheepskin coat and Stetson. My first thought was that something had happened.

"Is Rachel okay?"

"No, Yes." He sounded distracted.

"Which is it?"

"Yes, she's okay, I wanted to talk."

I couldn't let this man near me. He was everything I promised myself I didn't need, and the last thing I wanted to confront tonight. I pushed my key into the lock and turned it, opening the door a crack. It seemed as though Micah wasn't leaving.

"May I come in?" he asked.

"I don't think that's a good idea."

There was silence, with Micah staring beyond me to the front yard. Finally, I couldn't handle that silence, and huffed at my own stupidity.

"It's fucking ten below," I said tiredly, and stalked through the door, "Get the hell inside."

I wasn't in control of my actions, or my mouth, it seemed. I tensed when the door shut behind him and it was just the two of us in the wide empty hall. He checked it out, his hands in his pockets and his expression thoughtful.

"This place used to terrify us, you remember that?" If he was waiting for a reply it would be a long time coming. Obviously, he realized this and carried on, his tone a little desperate. He wanted me to engage, and I refused to.

"Doesn't seem so scary when you get inside," he murmured, then unbuttoned his jacket. I wanted to tell him to keep it on, but then he took off his Stetson and brushed his hair with his hand.

The action was so achingly familiar to me, I had to look away, taking off my outdoor clothes and kicking my boots to the side by the door. His hair was longer than usual, likely getting it cut wasn't high on his list of priorities, and he was tired, but all of that was way too much up in my space.

Mom didn't want me to ignore my feelings. She'd said I needed to come to some kind of peace for Chris' sake.

This was half on me.

I felt jumpy and uncomfortable in my own skin, as if anything I said now would expose the parts of me I wanted to hide from Micah. The fact that I'd been falling for him. I even had these stupid plans where he would be with me and we could buy this house together. He'd had a good job on the ranch, made it into something to be proud of. I was a doctor, or at least I'd been working my way towards being a doctor. I could have come home and made a life here for me and him.

How stupid was to have a life plan when you didn't really know the man you'd fallen for.

Running from my memories, fears, and the decisions I needed to make, I stalked into my decrepit empty kitchen and switched on the small coffee maker that made a maximum of two cups under protest.

"Scary in here though," Micah pointed out.

"Are you just here to comment on my house?" I snapped as I turned to face him. He was closer than I expected, almost looming. I think he realized it the same time I did, backing up until his ass hit the opposite wall.

"You said if I needed help you'd be there. Did you mean it? because I wanted to talk about Laurie, and Rachel."

"Patient confidentiality," I reminded him, as I waited for the coffee machine to do its thing.

"That's what I'm hoping for. I want to tell someone, and I guess you're the closest I have to a man who won't betray my trust. Because you're a doctor."

"You're not my patient."

He looked at me then, with absolute focus. "Then I have to trust you will do what is right." He ran his hand through his hair again, and this time he gripped the length of it and kept his hand there. I saw the way his body had changed since he'd left. I knew he'd been working on a ranch, could see the young man he'd been, but he was bigger now, broader, muscled, his stomach flat, his jeans riding low under his shirt. That had been the man I'd thought I could spend the rest of my life with.

"Can I?" he asked.

"Can you what?" The coffee machine spluttered and hissed and I made a mental note that I really needed to replace the damn thing.

"Trust you. I don't know why I'm asking, because that is all I can do right now. Details aren't important, but Rachel was trapped in…" he stopped, released the hold he had on his hair, his pale eyes bright with emotion, and I knew I could probably fill out the rest.

"An abusive relationship?" I offered.

He frowned and then nodded, as if he'd had to think

about that very hard, which made me think I wasn't being told the entire truth.

Still, he pressed on. "Laurie was hurt too, I think so anyway. He'd never been to a mall before, didn't like the noise or the crowds, the place they lived…"

I was getting frustrated with his lack of clarification in all of this, and I crossed my arms over my chest as he hesitated again. Then everything came out in a rush.

"If I'm not here, will you, as *their* doctor, and not for me but for them, make sure they get support?"

"It's my job." As a doctor that was an easy one to agree to, they were my patients.

Micah was suddenly defenseless, and the cold part inside of me felt a twinge of compassion. Then helpless was replaced by determined, as if he'd never shown a crack in his armor at all. He pushed back his shoulders.

"You said I shouldn't come back, I get that, but I'm staying as long as I can, so you'll have to deal with me being here." Then he turned to leave.

I shrugged as if I didn't care, even though I did, and changed the subject. "Chris told me you got to him. You want to tell me what did you and him talk about?" Maybe working myself up to anger would enable me to get Micah out of the house without revealing a single thing.

He stopped, but didn't turn back to me. "I didn't *get* to Chris, I talked to him."

"Why would he want to talk to you anyway?" Jesus, I should've stopped. What the hell was I doing? Besides feeling irrationally pissed that Chris and Micah had talked at all.

"That's between me and him," Micah said. He turned his back to me to and then despite my initial plans, there was no way I was letting him leave. I clenched my jaw and pain pressed at my temples. The anger that I had tried to summon finally took hold and all I could think was one thing.

What the fuck am I doing?

"You said you loved me, and then you ran!" I accused. Clearly, I was looking for confrontation. He stopped and pivoted to face me.

"You told me to go," he said, with wide eyes. "I loved you and you told me to go."

"You were nineteen, for God's sake. I might have been your first but I bet I wasn't your last."

There was nothing rational in my word.

"What the hell, Daniel?"

He moved backward and I knew I was stalking into him, the anger making its way to my fists. "You have a fucking skewed idea of love," I snapped.

He held up both hands when I was close. "Believe what you want, but back then, I imagined forever with you."

I couldn't help the noise of derision that escaped me, and noticed he'd tipped his chin and pushed his shoulders back again. He was going to argue with me. I stopped him before he could even try, and anger really had tucked itself into each word.

"You snuck out of my bed, took those keys. What were you thinking?"

Somehow, in everything that had happened since then, we'd never got to the why he'd done what he had. Maybe this was what I needed, to be able to close the door on what had happened, then possibly I would be okay.

"I wanted to prove I was a man," he said, softly, not

rising to my bad temper. His eyes were bright with emotion. As if maybe he'd cry.

"What?" I couldn't see what he meant with that explanation.

"My dad, he used to call me…" He shook his head, shaking free the memories maybe? "Look, that doesn't matter, we all know my dad changed after Mom died… He hated that I was spending time with you. A man. He wouldn't accept I was gay, told me he was changing the will to cut me off from the ranch. You know all that because I told you every single time you'd listen."

"Some parents are like that." I was being dismissive, but I wasn't sure who that was hurting. My parents had been supportive almost from the very first moment they knew. I got that not everyone had the same kind of parents as me.

Kids like Micah.

His hands clenched into fists. "You saw the fucking bruises," he said between gritted teeth.

"You argued with your dad, so is that your excuse for stealing my car and crashing it?"

"You know what he did to us, how he made us feel, as if we should have died instead of Mom."

He was devastated, and in a split second I recalled in vivid detail the day he'd come to the house with that damn cat. I remember the tears as he talked to Mom, about the cat, about his life, about what he wanted. All the things he couldn't have, and my anger left me in a rush. I couldn't sustain the anger with memories like that.

"Sorry, I know what that was like, I didn't mean to make it less than it was."

Great, now I'm adding insult to injury with a shitty

apology.

“Mom died, Rachel left for college, and it was just me, him, and the land.” He sagged a little, the wall the only thing holding him up. “My whole world was framed by his grief, and despair, and his refusal to listen to me, and understand *me.*” His eyes were bright with emotion and he was flushed. “Nine years and it seems like yesterday. Do you feel that sometimes?”

I had to be honest. “Yeah.”

“I was angry that morning. Dad was talking about selling the ranch. Not just the land, but the whole place. You know what he said? That there was no way he was leaving the place to Rachel and that I was dead to him because I was gay. He said over and over there was no difference between me and her, we were both *less than what he wanted*, and he hated that. You know, I was nineteen, and so damn mad, but in his own way he’d tapped into my own fears, that I was less of a man.”

"Jesus, Micah.”

He pushed ahead, not stopping to accept an ounce of understanding from me.

“That day, I left and I went to your house. I wanted to talk at first, but fuck, when I saw Chris all I wanted was to be the kid that your family loved. I didn’t tell him what my dad had said to me. He had beer, but I couldn’t even bring myself to drink to soften the bad temper.” He looked right at me, and all I could think was that he was exposing his entire heart to me. “All I wanted, what I *needed* was to see you. The man I loved, and who would smile at me, and treat me as if it was okay just to be me.”

“This all happened the day of the accident?”

When you came to my place over the garage and we

went further than we had ever done before.

"Yeah. I was desperate, and I wanted to show you that you meant everything to me, and that just being with you made sense." He closed his eyes briefly. "You remember I told you I loved you."

"I do."

"I was nineteen, I'd gone against my dad's wishes, had Chris laughing at me for wanting to be with his idiot older brother. God, so much in my head. Then, you were adamant that I couldn't know what love was, that what we'd done was just sex, and I felt…wrong. When you slept, all I could hear was my dad's voice, and then Chris, and you. I wasn't being what any of you wanted me to be, and I was a fucking kid, Daniel. I needed to be a kid, one last time. You said I could borrow the car at any time, so I held you at your word, and I took the keys to your car, and the rest…well you know what happened."

I couldn't believe what I was hearing and something in that mess of words hit a chord. "I know some of this is my fault."

Micah clenched his fists at his side, and I could see the effort it took him not to walk out now. "For fuck's sake," he snapped, and turned abruptly to leave. I followed him to the door as he opened it.

"Please, don't walk away from this discussion," I said.

He slammed the door shut and rounded on me. "What discussion? You're not fucking listening."

My temper snapped, I couldn't understand. I'd just admitted some responsibility, and he was shouting at me? He shoved me and I stumbled back to hit the wall.

"What the fuck, Micah—"

"You asked me why I took the keys, I spill every sorry

secret in my head, and you want to make it better by saying you'll take some of the blame? I lay out every ounce of my guilt and this is what you take from it?"

He poked my chest. I batted his hand away, but he persevered, then slammed his hand onto the wall next to my head.

"Not everything is about you making yourself feel better!" He shouted, inches from me, so close I could see his eyes in the dim lighting of my hallway. I could see the stubble on his face, the hint of gold in the blond, and I couldn't help myself. I reached out, grabbed him, and kissed him. No softness, no affection, this was pain and teeth and hurt. He didn't fight me at first and then he tried to pull away. I held tight, softened the kiss, wanted him to stay and kiss me like he meant it. I don't know what I was doing, why I had to taste him, why the reality of having him in my arms was everything I needed. I think I was stopping him from talking. Or apologizing. Or losing my fucking mind. All I knew is that the kisses grounded me.

For a brief time, the kiss became something real, because neither of us was in control. Micah moaned low in his throat, before finally pushing himself away. I tasted blood with my tongue. His blood. From where our kiss had opened up his healing split lip.

I was mortified, aroused, hurting, and blind to what I should be doing next.

"Micah?"

He reached for me then, placed a hand on my chest and pushed me gently so I was against the wall. Then he moved back in.

"Not like this," he murmured and kissed me gently, the softest sweetest kiss I had ever had, his soft tongue tracing mine, and his hand still flat over my heart. We kissed lazily, his tongue pressing at my lips until I opened my mouth, and tilted my head to deepen the kiss.

Then, before I could open my eyes and make sense of what had happened, he was gone. The door closing behind him.

For a long time, I stayed right there, as emotion after emotion buffeted me and left me unable to stand. I ended up sitting on the floor, and I pulled out my cell, looking for someone to talk me off the ledge. Could I use my family like that? I scrolled past Neil's name as well, and then hovered over Devin's name. He was a friend, my counselor. Maybe what I needed right now was a combination of both.

Because, fuck if I knew what was going on in my world. But, before I could connect to him, my phone rang and Chris' name flashed on the screen.

"Chris?"

"Michelle's in labor, and the midwife says she's close."

I put on shoes and coat, went to the car, realized I'd forgotten the keys, went back in for them, returned to the car, realized I'd forgotten the present for the baby that I'd wrapped a few weeks earlier. After another journey back to get my medical bag, just in case, I stopped, right on my porch. With the gift, keys, and medical bag in hand, I breathed to calm the hell down. Each breath was icy cold and hurt my lips, my throat, and down onto my chest, but I needed to ground myself. Until I felt I could hide the feelings the kiss had pulled to the surface.

Everything with Micah was out of control but I had a niece or nephew to meet, and that was the most important thing.

19

MICAH

I MADE IT OUT OF TOWN BEFORE I HAD TO PULL THE TRUCK to the side of the road and get out of the cab for air. The wind was biting, snow stinging any exposed skin, and I welcomed the pain of it for as long as my shame kept me hot.

Shame. Anger. Passion. Need. I wished to hell I could've split them apart and identified each one so I could work out how the hell I was. I kicked a tire, the thud a reassuring sound in the cold, then I kicked it again. My gloved hands in fists, I pounded on the hood, only stopping when I couldn't feel the pain anymore.

He kissed me.

Why had he forced that kiss on me, and then, how had I gone back in and let it become so much more than that?

I kissed him back.

Resting my hands on the door, I bowed my head, and tried not to relive every single second of it. I'd had nine years to forget the taste of him, or the way we fit together, but this was the second kiss. If I was honest with myself, there wasn't a single day that I didn't think of him in some small way. I should have shoved him away and left him standing there, drawn a line under the impossible.

But I hadn't. Not only had I not left, I'd kissed him for real, with passion and need and everything I had in me.

"Fucking hell!" I shouted in the snow.

Then, as if the fates hadn't messed with my head enough I saw the flash of lights and the cruiser that stopped back from me. I stared into the headlights, mesmerized by the snow that danced in front of them.

"Micah," Neil said as he came to stand next to me. He slapped his hands together and let out a puff of icy air. "You need help?" he asked as he gestured at my truck. I knew what he saw, a run-down heap of metal that was dead on the side of the road, and a man who was doing fuck all about it.

I needed help all right, but not the help that Neil could give me.

"Just needed air," I said, and regretted it. I should have implied I had broken down, or something that didn't invite questions.

Neil shrugged lower into his coat. "Saw you parked outside Daniel's place on my way in."

Great. Last thing I needed was a lecture on staying away from Daniel, or worse, some kind of formal opinion on what I'd done. I opened the car door, "I'll move her now." He stopped me with a gloved hand on my arm.

"You okay? He giving you a hard time?

Yeah. I was shoving him, and he kissed me, and split my lip again, but there was desperation in the kiss and I wanted more, so I stole what I needed from him and then left. And I'm not okay.

"I'm good, we just talked, reconnected. I need to go now if that's all, officer?"

Neil shook his head a little at that last part but didn't call me on it. He stepped away and when I looked back in my mirror he was getting into his own vehicle. I drove carefully on the icy roads, made it to the ranch and waited for a good five minutes, expecting him to appear behind me. There was no sign of him.

I went into the main house; it was only ten p.m. and the room in the bunkhouse, even with the heater I'd bought, was not a place to sit and warm up. There was coffee in the kitchen, and for a while I had the place to myself. At one point, Jeff appeared at the door, huffed at me as if I wasn't allowed to be in my own damn house, then left. I expected Amy to come out and tell me to leave them alone, but she didn't.

It was actually Rachel who came out, fully dressed, rubbing her temples. Laurie was close to her, in jeans, boots and his new thick coat.

"What's wrong?" Had someone from the compound found her? Was she asking us to leave? I was on my feet in a second, ready to run.

"Micah," she murmured. "I need to go to the hospital. There's blood."

She fell back against the door frame, before I could get to her, and I saw the blood, down her legs, soaking her dress. The crash pulled Jeff and Amy out, both of them furious, and likely thinking it was me causing a ruckus, but they immediately softened when they saw it was Rachel.

I was at her side in an instant, and she gripped me as hard as Laurie might've. I blinked at her in shock for a moment, and then everything happened at top speed.

Amy placed a hand on Laurie's head. "Go, we'll look after Laurie."

"No!" Laurie shouted.

"We'll take him with us," I said, and didn't wait for any arguments. I didn't want to leave Laurie here on his own, he needed his mom, and hell, he might even have needed me.

Somehow, I managed to get her to the car, scooping up Laurie into my arms, and buckling him into the new car seat. We had to drive through Whisper Ridge, and I almost stopped at Daniel's house, only Rachel hadn't said she needed a doctor, but that she had to get to the hospital. The bleeding wasn't stopping. She closed her eyes.

"Stay with me, Rachel, come on..."

I kept repeating the words, and in the back of the car Laurie was deadly silent.

When we skidded into the parking for Collier Springs Hospital I parked at the emergency door, and leapt out, slamming into the inside.

"I need some help here," I shouted, and everything happened at once. "My sister, she's pregnant and bleeding." She was pried from the car onto a gurney, the blood dark on her skirt, and staining the car. I unbuckled Laurie and held him so he couldn't see his mom, answering questions as best as I could. Her name, her age, the weeks she was pregnant, the bleeding, the headaches. Until abruptly I was in the corridor, and the silence was deafening. I couldn't go through the doors marked *Staff Only*, I couldn't hold her hand, and I couldn't make this right.

We all pay for our sins eventually. My father's voice in my head chilled me. Was Rachel paying for what I'd done all those years ago. Was this my fault? Or was it her because she'd killed a man. Maybe if I hadn't gone to Daniel's house then I would have been with her, able to help her as soon as the bleeding had started. Laurie squeezed me and I hugged him close and sat on the nearest chair.

"We have a family room," a kind nurse explained, but I wasn't moving away from this door and nothing the guy said was going to convince me, or Laurie, to move. Laurie was shaking, and I slipped off my coat and covered him with it, just as I had done on the porch that first day. He might just have been cold, or it may have been more, and I tried my best to comfort him, until finally he stopped shaking.

"Micah?" I looked up, needing it to be a doctor telling me what had happened, reassuring me that Rachel and the baby would be okay. It wasn't a doctor. It was Chris. "Is everything okay?"

I stared up at him, at the friend I'd once shared everything with. I wanted to tell him that Rachel was in the hospital, that she might be losing the baby, about the blood in my car, but I didn't. I wasn't able to form a sentence that would make sense.

Nothing made sense.

Chris nodded at me, then maneuvered to sit in the chair next to me, placing a hand on mine.

"We got this, buddy," he murmured.

He didn't even want to know what was wrong, he didn't care. He just knew I was here with my nephew, and he must have guessed it was Rachel. He said nothing, and the compassion he showed would have sent me to my knees if I didn't have Laurie in my arms.

"It's Rachel, she…"

"Yeah."

We sat in the quiet for a while, until Laurie wriggled out from under my coat.

"Where's Momma?" he asked me, and even though he gripped my coat hard he was staring at Chris.

"She'll be okay," I said, the white lie coming easily. I had every faith that she would be okay and I wouldn't be saying anything different where Laurie could hear me.

He turned on my lap and then clambered down, shrugging off my coat and his own, and then sitting on the small, comfy pile.

"Daddy said that Momma had the devil's baby," Laurie half whispered. "Is that why Momma's gone?" He looked so little sitting there, and my heart broke all over again. What kind of a man tells his son that a new baby was the Devil's? Next to me, Chris stiffened, and then pulled out his cell, firing off a text. I didn't want to know what he'd sent, probably something to the sheriff to tell him that there was a kid here talking about being the older brother to the devil's baby. I wanted to pick up Laurie, find Rachel, and take them all home to the ranch, hole up inside and keep them both safe.

"Your momma is going to have a beautiful baby," I said, and Laurie smiled at me.

"And my daddy is dead now anyway."

Jesus, any minute now and Laurie would be spilling everything. That couldn't happen. What did I say to him? How did I stop him? It was all going wrong.

"You have a metal leg," Laurie said, snapping me out of my spiraling thoughts, and then he knee-walked over to Chris and talked to him. "Are you a metal man?"

Two things struck me. The first was that a normal kid might have used the word robot, but maybe Laurie wasn't aware of that concept. The second was that Laurie was willingly talking to my old friend and not shying away from him. He'd also stopped talking about his dad, which I guess was the third thing.

"It's just my leg," Chris said, and pulled his pants leg up a little. I'd never seen it close like that; near enough to touch, and it was a complicated twist of metal that ended snugly in a shoe. "What's your name?" he asked. "I'm Chris."

"Laurence," Laurie murmured, but he was more interested in the leg than the fact he'd just given his name.

"Don't touch it, Laurie," I warned him and he glanced at me with a frown between his eyes before turning back to the shiny new thing he wanted to know about.

"It's okay, Laurie," Chris encouraged, picking up on the shortened version of my nephew's name. "You can touch it."

Laurie reached out and patted the prosthetic, and sat back, staring up at Chris expectantly. He clearly had a lot of questions, but they were forestalled when the staff door opened and the last man I expected to see walked out of the door. Daniel. He was grinning wide, obviously expecting Chris out in the hall, and not the man he'd just kissed. Unbidden, my fingers traced my cut lip, and I saw the moment he realized that Chris wasn't alone. His grin slipped, and he looked wary. He was a doctor, he seemed serious, and I put two and two together and made five.

I stood immediately, "Is Rachel okay? My sister? Is she okay?"

Daniel stopped, and pivoted on his heel to go back through the door. "I'll find out."

"That was Doctor Daniel," Laurie commented, still patting Chris's leg, as if he could memorize the shape of it for when he couldn't touch it anymore.

"If anyone can find out what's happening he can," Chris said.

"Okay." Then it hit me that Chris was here, in the hospital.

"We're all here for Michelle," he explained. "She's had a baby girl, and Daniel insisted that she came in, just to check the baby over." Chris didn't elaborate, I guess he was being respectful of the fact that there was something obviously wrong with my sister, when his own had just had a baby, probably surrounded by family, soft whale music and freaking candles. The door opened again and Daniel stood there hesitantly.

Chris saw him at the same moment as I did. "Hey Laurie, how about we go find something to eat?"

"No."

"Okay," he leaned down to Laurie. "How about the ranch. Do you like it there?"

Laurie peered at him through his long blond hair and frowned. "Horses," he said. Just the one word, but enough for Chris to get a hook.

"I love horses," he said, "Which one is your favorite?"

"The brown one," he said, and pushed his hair to one side.

"My favorite kind of horses are brown," Chris said.

"Cake," I prompted. Laurie scrambled to his feet and looked at me expectantly. "Chris will take you for cake if you want. I'll stay here."

"Can a metal man eat cake?" Laurie asked, and poked Chris' prosthetic to emphasize the question.

"Yes," Chris said, and grinned. "So much cake."

Laurie was uncertain, but then, as it was the way of many a kid, the lure of chocolate cake had him grasping Chris' hand and walking away with him. He glanced back once, tugged Chris to stop at least twice. I waved and grinned as if the world wasn't falling apart around me. As soon as he had gone around the corner, I stood and cut to the chase.

"Is she okay?"

"She's fine," Daniel said immediately, and then he gestured for me to follow him to a quieter corner. The corridor was empty but at least this gave the illusion of privacy.

"She's booked in for an ultrasound tomorrow," I said quickly, "and the midwife said everything seemed okay. What can I do? Why is she bleeding?"

Daniel held up a hand.

"Your sister has something called Placenta Previa, it's rare."

"Is the baby okay, is Rachel going to be okay, why was there so much blood, was she in pain?"

He paused, assessing whether or not he could tell me, and I couldn't help the anger that knotted inside.

He'd better tell me now, I'm all she has.

"I know it doesn't make sense, but severe, uncontrollable bleeding can happen without any pain. If Rachel had an ultrasound at twenty weeks it might have shown cause for concern, but I know she didn't have one. We would have recommended bed rest, but it's too late for that." He cupped a hand on my shoulder. "They're suggesting a cesarean to stop excessive life-threatening bleeding for Rachel and lack of oxygen for the baby. She's awake for now though, competent to make her own choice to have it done, but she wants to see you."

I knew about problems in pregnancy in horses—that was my arena, birthing foals, dealing with the issues, but this? Hell, this was my sister, and her baby, and now she wanted to talk to me? What was I going to say? Of course, she should have a cesarean if it would save her and the baby, but what if it was too late? Everything must have been telegraphed on my face. Daniel watched me go through the entire thought process.

"Everything will be okay," he said gently, and patted my arm, then led me through and left me.

The room Rachel was in was clean and neat and full of machines. There was no blood now, or at least none I could see, but she had a drip and a nurse was writing something on a clipboard before fiddling with buttons on a monitor. Rachel smiled at me when I walked in, the first time I'd seen a genuine smile on her face since I'd taken her from the compound.

Once the nurse left it was just the two of us. When we were kids I would sometimes go into her room to talk to her when things were really bad. Like when Mom died, or when Dad was drinking. The last time we'd really talked was the day of the accident, right after I'd argued loudly with our dad about everything that festered between us. She'd been in her first semester at college and she wanted to stay for the trial, I told her I didn't want here there. She'd returned to college, and hell, I was glad she'd listened to me and hadn't seen it. That one call I made to her with the number of my crappy phone, was the only connection we had. I'd never come back to Whisper Creek and neither had she.

Somewhere along the way, we had lost that brother-sister link and I hated that our family had ended up that way. Her white-blonde hair was scraped back from her face, and she looked tired, but peaceful.

"You have to promise me something," she said, and held out a hand, which I took.

"Anything," I said, emotion choking my voice.

"If something happens to me, you take Laurie and you make a life for him."

I rocked back on my heels as if she had slapped me. "Nothing is going to happen to you."

She forged ahead with determination. "I don't have a will, or family other than you, and I want you to fight for Laurie if they try to take him away from you."

"Jesus, Rachel—"

"Laurie, and the baby, both of them. Promise me." Her tone was fierce, and hell, it was an easy promise to make, they were as much my blood as she was.

"Of course, there is no reason to ask me."

"And you'll tell the police what really happened at the compound with Callum. You tell them it was me, if anything happens."

I nodded, but nothing was going to hurt Rachel. I wouldn't let it.

I left the room when the nurse came in, my head spinning with what I had just promised and how vital it was to make everything right. Daniel was right outside, waiting for me and I stopped in front of him, not knowing what to say. He reached out to cup my face and I let him, because I needed that touch desperately. I leaned into his touch and waited for him to say something, or to move. Anything. He gathered me in for a hug, and held me close, and everything came flooding back. I'd needed him when I was nineteen, that safe place where I could be who I wanted to be, and now, at twenty-eight, I needed him again.

The decisions I'd made? The mistakes? None of those meant anything when I was in his arms, and all I wanted to do was cry.

Only when I sat outside the room, with Laurie on my lap, waiting for something to go right for my sister, did I finally acknowledge that bad things always seemed to happen to the Lennox family.

Laurie had to have a different life.

20

DANIEL

I HUNG AROUND THE HOSPITAL AND KEPT AN EYE ON Rachel, even after Michelle had gone home after her brief checkup. I didn't think she'd forgive me for making her go the hospital after my beautiful niece, Abby, was born, but I was adamant I wanted them both checked out.

I fully understand why my family thought I was being neurotic, but I'd seen too much death in the emergency room and Michelle, bless her heart, indulged my stupidity. I think she saw it as *handling my PTSD;* I saw it as being medically safe.

Rachel was still in her room though, and three nights before they'd had to perform a cesarean. The doctors and midwives on call had given her corticosteroids to speed up the development of her baby's lungs, and managed to stem the bleeding, but at thirty-six weeks the baby had to be born. The little boy arrived quietly, was whisked away for checks, and Rachel cried through most of it.

Not that I was there. Micah told me this. He spent a lot

of time going between the ranch and the hospital and looked exhausted. Scott told me that Micah was working all hours with a crew to fix several years of neglect in the far reaches of the property. Fences were being mended and a rockfall shored up. All of this was being done in bitter weather, with snow permanently on the ground, and there was a feeling of desperation that I got from Micah whenever I saw him. I pretended that I didn't want to know the details from Scott, but I actually needed to hear everything.

And I saw him a lot. Like now for instance; I knew where to find him. It was lunchtime and he'd be in Rachel's room, with Laurie in tow, and food for Rachel that he'd bought from home. Laurie had become used to the hospital now, his own small corner of his mom's room laid out for jigsaws. I always crouched to help him, but he wouldn't let me do much, so I would restrict interaction to handing him a piece that I thought fit. I talked to Rachel, but I wasn't there for long and she seemed focused on her new son, who she'd called Oliver, and on Laurie. Sometimes Scott would be there, and he made Rachel smile, hell, Laurie had even talked to him, which I was refusing to be jealous about.

Because, hey, I was a grown up, and way too old to be jealous of one of my brothers.

I'd taken to visiting the hospital in my long lunch hour, which was something I had the luxury of having. I recalled shifts in the ER where I didn't eat for a day, and I made a mental note as I finished the last of my sandwiches that I should up my exercise to counteract this. Maybe I could take up running, or just spend hours walking up from the basement to the attic in my house. Four flights of stairs and

I could think about improvements I wanted to make at the same time.

Baby Oliver was a healthy six pounds, and Rachel was lucky enough to have avoided the worst of the post-partum low. Unlike Michelle, who'd cried at an episode of *The Simpsons* and announced she was done having children. I'd seen that kind of thing before, and I knew Michelle, as soon as she was better she'd want another. Still, I kept a close eye on her, because sometimes the blues stayed far longer than they should. Between me and Mom, we fussed over her, and sent her to sleep until Rick, her husband and doting dad, arrived home from work. Best Sunday ever because I got to hold my niece, Abby, for a good hour of cuddles.

When I saw Micah holding Oliver, talking to Rachel, I stopped in my tracks. Between one thing and another, I hadn't seen Micah actually holding the new arrival. The baby was so tiny in his arms, and he was relaxed.

I stepped inside.

"Doctor Daniel!" Laurie called to me, his little face breaking into a smile. "We're going home, all of us."

I glanced at Micah who nodded, and a great wash of disappointment had me thinking about just how invested I was in this little family. What was it about Rachel and Laurie that made me care, and Oliver, why did I hope he'd have a better start than Laurie had?

Because I'm a normal human being with compassion. Doesn't mean anything else.

Then there was Micah. Why did I care about his welfare? It worried me that he was tired and drawn, unshaven and his hair longer than I had ever seen it. I knew I would miss seeing them in my lunch hour.

"That's wonderful," I said, with as much fervor as I could. Micah narrowed his eyes at me, and then frowned at my forced enthusiasm. "Anyway, bye." I backed out of the room, and headed out before they asked me why I was going, aiming right for the staff parking lot hidden from the hospital by a bank of chokecherry trees. I was almost in the car, had the door open, when Micah stopped me.

"I've had enough of your shit," he snapped, and I turned to face him. He looked murderous, and stubborn, and still exhausted. "I'm going soon, so don't the fuck take your shit out on my sister or the kids."

I heard the words, but genuinely felt lost. I'd gone in, said hello, said goodbye, and that was me pretty much done there. What the hell was Micah going on about?

"What?" I said, and he stepped up into my space. I wished he wouldn't do that to me, it was unnerving and arousing and a thousand other bad things between.

"Rachel is a damn good mother."

"I'm sure she is."

He poked at me, and I took it that time. "You know her fucker of a husband used to beat her, and I bet he wasn't the only one, and I know she took it if it meant he left Laurie alone."

"Micah—"

"So, you can look disappointed that she's finally getting to go home, or worry that you don't get to watch her twenty-four seven, asshole. But she will work damn hard for her family, and she'll be just as good a mom as your sister, and you will not comment on this or mess with her, or look like the baby is fucked over for life because of what you think about me. Okay?"

He was in a bad mood, I could see it even over the

exhaustion, but he'd misread everything, and my reaction had broken something inside of him. He poked at me again, as if that was going to underline his words.

I captured the finger and held it.

"Stop poking me," I said, as calmly as I could. I was trapped there, against my car, with Micah up close. "I'm disappointed she's going home because I liked visiting, seeing them, Laurie, you. When you're back at the ranch—that will be it, no more."

He looked uncertain and moved a little away from me. I didn't let go of his finger, instead I laced my fingers with his. I pressed ahead. "Rachel obviously loves her children, and has managed to escape from a horrible situation, with your help, to try and start over. I admire her, and hell, I'm amazed at the kind of brother you are to her."

He unlaced his fingers, and I knew I'd said that wrong. What I was saying was coming from a point in me that still held anger at what he'd done nine years ago, but along with it was some understanding, forgiveness, peace.

"Okay," he said, with a shrug, accepting what I had just said, and taking it the wrong way because he didn't understand what was in my head. Of course, he couldn't, I hadn't explained any of it properly. Maybe it was time to be specific about what I was trying to say.

But not there. Not then.

"Can you come to the house? I thought we should…no, I'd like to talk."

I waited for him to tell me to get lost, but he didn't. He was thoughtful and put his hands into his pockets. We were sheltered there, but the wind still bit, and he'd come out without his coat.

“Okay,” he said, after a while. “Scott is coming to the ranch this evening. I’ll come over after.”

My car was a quiet place for me to have a private meltdown, and I still had another twenty minutes left to get back to Whisper Ridge. I called Devin, made an appointment and went back to work.

The afternoon was slow, and by the time five came around I was ready to go, heading back to Collier Springs and to the offices where Devin held his clinic.

I was lucky that Devin had an appointment available when everything was raw in my head. He shook my hand, shut the door on us, and abruptly I lost all the thoughts I’d had, all the whys and wherefores, all the reasons why I was spiraling on all of this.

"How have you been?” Devin sat back in his chair. In our sessions we talked about inconsequential things to start, the weather, sports, then onto family, before we finally hit the main points of why I was there.

"Daniel?” Devin prompted.

Everything slammed back into me with such a force that it was as if I couldn’t stop. I told him all I could, and it was a torrent of self-recrimination, guilt and panic. Then there was the kiss. I talked about the kiss in detail and what I thought it meant to me.

He listened, and then, when I’d finished, he leaned forward.

“You want my advice?” he asked.

“That’s what I’m paying you for.” I laughed, more with nerves than anything else. I’d told him everything, from falling in love, to betrayal, to despair, to fear, and it all lay between us.

“You say that Micah told you why he did what he did,

and then there was the kissing, the second of which you described as angry, and then not angry."

"Yep."

"Now it's your turn to tell him everything, just like you have me," Devin said. "You need to tell him why you felt betrayed, why everything hurt, and about what happened to you a few months ago in Charlotte. You need to say it all rationally, and I know it's hard because it's all mixed up with the incident with the gunman. At the end of the day it's really simple, Daniel, do you want to tell him everything you just told me?"

Do I?

"Yes. I do."

21

DANIEL

The knock came just after eight, and my heart quickened with nerves and anticipation in equal measure. I let him in, took note that he'd dressed up for his meeting with Scott, good jeans, a shirt, and he'd shaved, although he'd left his hair alone, not shaving it back to near-nothing.

I hung up his jacket, and we made small talk as we went into the kitchen for me to make coffee. I pulled out what was left of Mom's latest cake, some kind of chocolate layer cake with vanilla frosting, and cut Micah a piece.

"Did it go okay with Scott?"

He picked up the cake and coffee, "You're invested in Scott's business."

"Oh, then we all are, all five of us."

"So, you'll know what he offered, and I accepted the price, passed over the signed contract." He sounded tense, and it must hurt to let some of his land go, given how fiercely he had loved the place as a kid.

"Is that what you really wanted? I'm sorry if we're

benefiting from Rachel needing the money." I meant it sincerely.

"It's business, and actually, yeah, I'm good with it. The ranch needs the influx of cash to keep it steady, and there's no point in hanging onto something that we may never use." He sighed heavily. "It's all good."

There was the perfect opening for the first of my questions. "I know you worked on a ranch, tell me again what you did?"

He looked down at his cake for a moment and then back up at me. "You mean, you want me to explain again how I could send back so much money for the upkeep of the ranch?" He didn't sound defensive, more resigned to the question being asked. Before I could insist that wasn't what I meant he kept talking. "I was a partner in a horse training concern, worked with kids, didn't need much, so invested most of my income back into Lennox Ranch, with a sum in savings, to keep it for Rachel."

I picked up the fact that he didn't include himself in that. He was a cowboy at heart, rough and ready, but the land was his, and I couldn't imagine him giving it up for one moment.

"That is a lot more boring than the money being drug-related," I quipped, and then wondered if that was a step too far. He grinned then, wide and open.

"Maggie Gentry stopped me by the store, asked me if I'd spent the last nine years in porn."

"Maggie Gentry is an idiot," I reassured. The old woman was easily confused, but that didn't mean the rumor of Micah selling himself for money hadn't made the rounds, along with the concept that he'd become a spy. I guess the townsfolk were just hunting for reasons as to how he'd managed to send so much money back.

"Well, it definitely wasn't porn," he said, and lifted his plate a little. "Are we taking this into the other room?"

Coffee and cake in hand we sat opposite each other.

"Your mom's cakes were always so good." He cut off a small piece and pushed it to one side of the plate, just like the Sheridan siblings did. For Mom. The same woman who had been there for Micah.

"She's not here," I said, and he glanced up at me, confused.

"What?"

I tipped my fork at his plate. "You've left the bit for Mom."

He smiled then, poking at the small piece. "It's habit I guess, something I always do." His smile was just what I remembered, and the fact that he was lost in memories made his expression soften. For a moment I saw the nineteen-year-old sitting opposite me.

"I remember how I felt when you said you loved me," I blurted out, and his smile vanished and he was pained instead. "I remember being so pissed at you."

That was entirely the wrong thing to say and I waited for him to run. He tensed but he didn't move.

"I don't care, it was what I felt."

"I know, but I had my entire life mapped out for me, I was going to be a doctor, intern in a hospital, bring skills home. Nowhere did that include falling for a man who might make me stay at home. But when I woke up that evening, and you'd gone, I was disappointed in myself. I was determined to find you and tell you I loved you back."

Silence. Micah put the plate on the coffee table

between us, and I knew he'd have something to say, but I pressed ahead while I still could.

"Then I saw you'd taken the car, but it was still okay, because I said you could borrow it any time, and it felt good that my boyfriend was sharing my things, that the man I loved was such an integral part of my life. You hadn't stolen the car, you'd borrowed it, and it made me happy." I swallowed the emotion balling inside me, and Micah was pale, his mouth slightly open.

"When you said to them I'd stolen it, I was happy you said that."

"I should have told the truth—"

"I deserved prison time—"

We spoke at the same time, and abruptly stopped.

"I should be thanking you," I said, because the words were inside choking me. "Thanking you for pulling Chris from the car. The firefighters said he would have died in the fire, trapped, but you went back into the car," I touched my wrist to indicate his own burns. "So, thank you for risking your life for my brother."

"I put him in that situation—"

"That was the first thing," I interrupted, because I had a lot more to say. "I loved you, thank you for saving my brother, and I'm sorry for what I did to you, making you leave, because you deserved the support to cope with your own grief. I made you go and you lost my family as decisively as losing your own mom."

He shook his head as if he couldn't agree with what I was saying.

"I'm confused," Micah murmured. "What I did to your family, to Isaac—"

"You didn't do that yourself, it was an accident. I

carried the feelings of hate and betrayal around for so long, and it was even worse when I found Chris unconscious with the pill bottle next to him."

"He told me what he did."

"Yeah, Chris had a dark time, when he first came home."

"I'm sorry." The guilt was back in his voice.

"I think, for Chris, it was a way of resetting his brain. When he woke up I remember him holding my hand and telling me he didn't want to die. It was a turning point."

"He had so much he could have done."

"You know I was just as much a part of everything that happened, even if I wasn't in the damn car. If I had been able to imagine a future with you, if I'd thought I was strong enough for us to stay together and just told you how I really felt all that time ago."

He frowned again, and I could see his internal battle telegraphed on his expression. "But, if I hadn't stolen the car…"

"Borrowed, and if I hadn't taught you and Chris to drive." I was teasing, but with hindsight now was not the best time to bring any lightness into this. I'd blindsided Micah with the results of a lot of internal evaluation and this was some serious shit.

"Don't make this a fucking joke," he said and stood in a flurry of motion, "all this fucking time."

Shit. I was losing him, and I stood as well.

"Wait, there's one more thing. Lastly, I don't think, under it all, that I ever stopped loving you either."

That was the final admission, and it hung there between us waiting for him to react. I walked around the table and held out a hand, and after a moment of hesitation he took it. I laced our fingers, and then took his other hand.

"I've never wanted anyone else as much since, I've never loved anyone else as completely. I'm sorry I didn't fight for you. I'm sorry I wouldn't tell the cops I said you could borrow the car. They said it made no difference to your defense, but if I'd stood up for you, then you would have known things could be okay one day."

The guilt blooming inside me was enormous, and I waited for some sign that he understood my remorse, and that I'd been as much of a kid as he'd been. We'd wasted so much time and I wanted it back.

"What now?" He stepped toward me, dropping my hands as he moved. I could hug him, hold him and, maybe through touch, we could somehow have everything make sense.

Instead I waited, and he pressed a soft kiss to my lips.

"I need time to think. I'm not sure we'll ever be anything to each other. What would people think?"

My stomach sank. I'd wanted hope, but it seemed as if I wasn't going to be lucky enough to get that. He backed away and left my front room and I waited for the sound of him putting his coat on, his boots, and the crash of the front door. There was nothing, and I imagined him standing there thinking over what I'd said. Should I go to him? I stared down at the dark brown and orange carpet, threadbare and old, and followed the patterns to where they vanished under the sofa.

I sensed Micah back in the room, at the door. "Fuck what people think." He spoke firmly. He'd made a decision and he was done. I looked up at him, waiting for him to say that it had been too long, that there had been too much anger and hate between us.

We moved at the same time, I wondered if I was going to beg him to stay, or accept that he was leaving, when he took me in his arms and kissed me. Not harsh, not to punish, but more kissing, soft but determined.

Cradling my face, Micah tilted his head and deepened the kiss and it was a match to tinder. He was calling all the shots and I was happy to be taken along for the ride. We broke apart and for the longest moment we just stared at each other, but I couldn't fail to notice he was breathing as hard as I was. We met again in the middle, kissing, only stopping to walk out of the front room, and to the stairs. We kissed on every step and with each inch of climb we fought to rid ourselves of clothes, and then gave up when we nearly fell down the damn stairs.

Could we have uncomplicated sex after what I'd just said, and what Micah had admitted to me? Wasn't love complicated enough?

"This is going to be so fucking complicated," he murmured against my lips. Then he stopped and pulled back. "I'm still leaving town," he said, and even though the words broke something inside of me, I chose not to linger on them. I was a man, and I wanted Micah, and it didn't matter what happened *tomorrow* when *today* I had him here in my arms.

I kissed him, left him in no doubt that it didn't matter what he said, we were doing this, and after a short hesitation he kissed me back. That was all the talking we needed.

22

MICAH

Daniel pushed me onto the bed, and I didn't fight it, falling back but making sure to hook his shirt and bring him down with me. He stole a kiss before I could move, and I heard myself moan into it. I attempted to move my hands, but Daniel laced them together and held me there, using his knee to nudge my legs apart and then lying across me, letting his weight pin me to the bed. He was hard against me and I was so turned on I could barely get my thoughts together before I instinctively rutted up against him.

The kisses became more, as Daniel spent a long time kissing my neck and then back up to my lips, murmuring words I couldn't even hear. I wanted skin, and I needed it. I pulled my hands free of his to grip his ass, pushing up as he ground down against me. The desperation level rose exponentially, and I yanked at fabric, until I could touch his back, tracing the warmth of it.

He mumbled something into the kiss, and I backed up a little.

"What?" I asked.

He moved off me and my chest tightened. Was he going to reject me now, tell me we weren't a thing that would ever happen? I couldn't have been more wrong, he began to undress, wriggling on the bed, getting his foot caught in his jeans and boot, and I half rolled onto him.

"Wait," I instructed, and slid my hand down his body to his pants, which had bunched at his feet. I helped him out with them, his boots, jeans, boxers, all gone, and then I climbed his body. It was my turn to nudge his legs apart, pressing my knee against his balls, as I unbuttoned his shirt. The cloth parted easily and I pushed it down his arms and then I stopped. With his arms stuck, I had him pinned and I leaned over him, licking and biting his nipples, gripping his shirt so he couldn't move. He squirmed and cursed and sighed, and only when he pressed against my knee mewling did I let him slip the shirt off.

Then it was on. He flipped us easily, because there was nothing I wanted more than to be under him. He was a toppy bastard, always had been when it came to sex, and muscle memory took over. I could've pushed him to the edge until he snapped but then, at the end of it, he would be the one fucking me.

I was still dressed, although I'd toed off my boots with a struggle and my pants were looser. Then he began to remove layer by layer, and every time he moved he kissed me, licked a trail of kisses from nipple to navel and then lower. He circled my cock and moved a little so he was biting my hip bones, soothing the hurts with kisses, tasting every part of me. He nudged at my cock and licked the length of me.

"Watch me," he instructed and I pushed myself up on

my elbows as he tugged me to the edge of the bed. He went to his knees, and firmly pressed my legs apart, just looking. Just when I thought I would snap and ask him to suck me, he began to lick my cock and push down on my thighs. I couldn't move again and he could do what he wanted to me.

"God. Daniel," I whispered, watching his head bob, seeing my cock vanish into his mouth, the suction perfect…and his tongue. He always could bring me to the edge just like this and I couldn't keep myself up any more, falling back on the mattress. When I was so damn close I had to warn him, he climbed onto the bed and caged me, leaning down and kissing me. I reached up to press a hand to the back of Daniel's head.

I need more kisses.

He reared back. "No," he growled and I loved that. He would pretend to control everything, and fuck if that didn't turn me on. He reached to his bedside cabinet, and pulled out whatever he needed, squirted lube onto my belly and chuckled at my gasped protest. His tongue darted out to dampen his lips and I couldn't take my eyes off of him. He smoothed the lube on his finger, kissing me, and slid his hand under my balls, the wet cold enough for me to gasp again.

"Is this okay?" he asked me, concerned, and there was no way I was letting him stop now.

"Fuck me," I demanded.

He looked so serious, pressing his fingers right there, and pushing inside, with more lube and determination.

It had been so long, and yeah, I'd had sex since Daniel, but this was *Daniel*. I needed him like I needed to breathe.

“I want to fuck you so bad,” Daniel moaned, and kissed me, “taste all of you.”

I arched up and he stopped kissing me and placed a warning hand on my belly, but I showed him my intent when I pushed down on his fingers, and he groaned.

“Now,” I ordered, and then added a please, because I knew he would slow things down if I started telling him what to do.

He bit my earlobe, “I’ll get you there,” he promised and I nearly came right then.

He moved back, wiped his hand on his discarded shirt and rolled on a condom.

“On your front,” he demanded, and I hurried to roll over, this was always the best way, not quite on all fours, but enough so he could grip me and fuck me hard. "Jesus, Micah, you should see yourself. So beautiful.” He pressed inside, slowly, until finally he was in, and the rhythm he set was desperate. My cock was touching the covers, the soft material rubbing me. I couldn’t get enough friction, and the bastard wouldn’t let me move lower, or go more upright to get a hand on myself.

It was always this way. How could I have ever forgotten how hot sex was with Daniel?

I groaned.

“Am I hurting you?” he asked, desperately.

“No, harder.”

At that he set a punishing rhythm but I wasn’t getting close enough to come and I told him, I asked him, I freaking begged him to get his hand on me. Finally, he lifted me to all fours, the angle just perfect, so right, and he leaned over me.

“Touch yourself, get yourself off, beautiful man.”

I tried, it took a while to balance while Daniel fucked me, but finally I had my hand on myself, and he warned me he was close, and I lost it, a few twists of my hand and I was coming over the covers, with him finishing deep inside me just after.

We ended up in a hot sweaty heap, tangled together so I couldn't tell where I ended and he began.

"You said you were leaving," he whispered. "I'll make you stay, show you we can do this. Together."

I made a noise of agreement, too fucked out to argue. I knew I'd take his words and dissect them when I was on my own, but for now, all I wanted to do was sleep.

"Do you remember the first time we kissed?" he asked as I was close to sleep. I turned in his arms and he held me close.

"Always," I said. "Always."

I woke to sunlight breaking through a crack in the drapes, and watched Daniel sleeping.

I'd said I was still leaving. It was just sex. I love him but it can't be anything else, not if I have to go to protect my family.

I dressed as quietly as I could, and left a note propped up by the coffee maker where he was sure to see it. It was short and to the point.

'Had to go, sorry. Talk later. M.'

There wasn't much to it as notes go, not that he'd been expecting hearts and flowers, but it was more than enough to make me smile that I'd left it.

23

MICAH

THE FENCE SEPARATING OUR LAND FROM WHAT WOULD BE Sheridan-owned acreage was nearly finished. We'd tried to make it as sturdy as possible, working long hours to get it done. When the team of workers went home, after the snow refused to ease up, it was just me out there walking the length of the fence toward the bridge, before heading back up the hill to the ranch. A car drove up the road, but I was too far away to see who it was, and didn't recognize the vehicle at all.

I admit at first my heart had leaped a little at the thought that it could be Daniel. After I'd gone, leaving the note, I'd landed in chaos. Oliver took up a lot of my down time, as did Laurie, and then add in ranch work and it had been three days since I'd seen Daniel and I wondered how he was feeling about what we'd done. He hadn't been out to visit, in fact his dad had completed the welfare check, pronouncing mom and baby as doing well.

We'd chatted for a while but not about anything personal, and we were respectful of each other. He'd even shaken my hand when he left and told me he was glad to see me back.

It even sounded as if he'd meant it.

I finally reached the ranch house, after quickening my steps, after all there was a stranger on our land. What I saw didn't leave me at ease. Jeff was at the door, with it closed behind him and a rifle in his hand. In front of him was the figure of a man, but all I could make out from this distance was that he had dark hair and was tall. I quickened my pace into a jog, and finally ended up between Jeff and the stranger.

"Can I help you?" I said politely, "Put the gun away, Jeff."

Jeff muttered something about idiot fools, but clomped into the house and slammed the door.

"I'm here to talk to Rachel Prince."

I hid my fear, Prince was Rachel's married name. Who would be there looking for her?

"And you are?" I crossed my arms over my chest, and tried to appear threatening, but this guy was taller by six inches and outweighed me considerably. He was muscled and strong and every bit as intimidating as I was trying to be.

"My card," he said and held it out. I didn't move, and I certainly didn't take the damn card. "Does Rachel Prince live here?"

"And I say again, who the hell are you?"

"Someone who really needs to talk to Rachel Prince."

We were at an impasse. Obviously. If the guy had been a cop he'd have flashed a badge by now, surely.

"Rachel Prince doesn't live here."

The door opened behind me and Rachel called my name questioningly "Micah?"

I didn't turn around. "Go back in the house."

The big man's eyes widened. "Rachel Prince? Can we talk?"

"Get. Back. In. The. House." I insisted and she did, thank God.

We stared at each other, and I think if he'd wanted to he could've taken me down, walked right over me to get to my sister. I tensed in readiness for a fight.

"Please," he murmured, and it was as if someone had cut his strings, there was grief in his expression, and passion. When I didn't respond he nodded, as if he understood what I was doing. "I'll be staying in Collier Springs, at the Mennier Bed and Breakfast." He sighed and turned to walk away, stopping and facing me again.

"What?" I fronted.

"My cousin, Natalie, died at that Brothers of Chiron compound eight years ago," he said, and then he turned to leave again. The news shocked me —that the reason he was here wasn't to find Rachel to interrogate her, but to connect her to his cousin.

Cracking my neck, I decided this wasn't done, and that I needed to talk to him. I had to have some better idea of what was happening, so I followed the guy to the car, away from the relative safety of the house and Jeff's rifle.

I extended my hand, "Micah Lennox. I'm Rachel's brother."

He shook it warily. " Connor Mason. Private investigator."

"What do you want from us?"

It looked to me as if he was evaluating what to say to

me, and that was dangerous. I couldn't handle dishonesty, not right now, with my sister's safety in the balance.

"I'd like to talk to your sister, if I can."

"No."

He regarded me steadily and then closed his eyes, and I saw that same naked grief back in his expression. "They found my cousin's body ten miles away in a creek and the cops couldn't connect her to the compound, but that was where she was. She contacted me, told me she wanted to leave, that she was scared, I wasn't as lucky as you, when I got to where we were supposed to meet, she wasn't there. I was too late."

I'd seen deception in my life. This wasn't it. There was raw honesty in his words and I trusted my gut that he wasn't there to harm us.

"How did you find Rachel?"

He studied the house.

"Surveillance," he said, when he turned back. "A concerned parent hired me to find his son."

"And the son was there with Rachel?"

"Yes."

I remembered the shadows in the dark. "A child?"

"No."

The biting wind was more than the PI seemed able to handle. Judging from his tanned skin he was more used to sun than snow, and he shivered in his thick coat.

"What do you think Rachel can help you with?"

He sighed, and closed his eyes briefly, as if he had the weight of the world on his shoulders. "Hope. That's all I'm looking for. Just hope." His green eyes were bright with emotion. I could share that need. Hope is all we can ever ask for in life.

"Come with me."

I took him through the barn to my bunkhouse room and told him to wait, before going back to the house and finding Rachel. She was in the bedroom, tucking a sleeping Laurie into bed for a nap.

"I think we should talk to him, find out what he wants."

She looked at me as if I'd lost my mind, and maybe I had, but there were too many secrets, and if surveillance had led him to Rachel, then who knew what other people might have the intel. If we could find out what he had, reason with him, then maybe Rachel would stay safe.

"Micah, are you sure?"

She picked up Oliver, wrapped in a blanket and waited for me to explain why I even thought talking to a stranger was a good idea.

"We need to be certain about what he knows, sis."

She took that at face value, and we wrapped Oliver up even more and walked over to the barn. I took Oliver from her and she followed slowly.

"Thank you, this means so much." Connor stood, but I had one warning for him.

"Understand that I'm staying, and I will stop this if it's too much."

He nodded.

Seemed like we had a deal.

THE THREE OF us sat in a loose circle in the small room, the two heaters on full blast. At least this way we were out of the house and away from Amy and Jeff, and I hoped Laurie stayed sleeping. Amy said she'd keep an eye out for him, and I could tell she was desperate to know what was going on, but I didn't enlighten her. Not yet.

Connor was polite and calm, exhibiting none of the stress he'd shown earlier, with a list of questions and one photo that looked like it had been in a wallet or something, given how battered it was. I wondered if maybe there was more to this story than a PI searching for the son of a senator. He'd mentioned his cousin, but not the identity of the man he'd been searching for. I guess that was part of his contract, that he kept that knowledge to himself.

He showed Rachel the picture of a dark-haired man. She went pale and her eyes filled with tears.

"Max," she murmured. "He helped us. I didn't see him when we left. I don't know if he was still at the compound, or if he left as he said he was. I don't know where he is. I'm sorry."

Connor deflated but he kept a professional hold on the situation. "Can you tell me anything about what he was doing, or anything he might have said to you?"

She shook her head and Oliver stirred in her arms. He caught her thumb in his tiny hand and the fanciful side of me thought maybe he was supporting his momma.

"I wasn't allowed to talk to him, but he was new, a convert, or that is what I was told. The day before I left, he was the one who found me and told me to run if I could. He gave me his phone, and I called Micah for help. That was the last time I saw Max."

"I don't suppose you still have the phone?" Connor asked with a glimmer of optimism in his voice.

"No, I hid it."

Connor's hope was dashed. "Then, it burned with everything else then."

"What burned?" she said and turned to me as if I knew. I shook my head, he hadn't told me that, and there was still nothing in the news despite how many times I checked.

"Someone set the compound on fire, the main building anyway."

"The children?" Rachel was white, and I shuffled closer to hold her and Oliver. "There were children, are they okay?"

He shook his head, "I don't know who survived and who died. I wish I did."

I could see he was lying, but at that moment I didn't want Rachel to hear any truths about people she may have known dying, particularly the children she'd talked about. At least Rachel believed him, and that was all that mattered. When he looked at me I gave a small nod of thanks and he nodded back.

"The phone was in the washrooms, if they burned, then yes, it's gone."

Connor opened the folder and began to pull out a picture of the gutted buildings, and I thought I saw bodies in the foreground so I stopped him with a touch to his hand. "No photos."

He flushed with embarrassment. "Shit, I'm sorry, I didn't think."

"I wish I could help you more," Rachel rocked Oliver, and her eyes were bright. I thought she might cry. "Max was a kind man, I could never understand why he was there at all."

"It's a long story," Connor murmured.

Before he left, his folder close to his chest, he shook my hand, and gave us his card, which I took this time.

"Thank you," he said simply, and we both watched him drive away.

Rachel leaned on me, and together we went back in the house, Oliver was fast asleep in her arms, and we let ourselves into the kitchen as quietly as we could so as not to wake Oliver. I followed her to her room, walking straight past Jeff, who was clearly looking for answers. I held up a hand to indicate five and he turned back to Amy, who was in the pantry.

Rachel hugged me in relief, but I was worried. If one man could track Rachel down, link her to what happened…then what if that surveillance showed others what had happened, or who'd been there?

"It will be okay," Rachel said, and tucked Oliver into his bassinet.

"How Rachel? If one person can find us, then what's to stop them connecting us to what we did to Darren Prince? How can we hide that we killed him?"

The startled sound from behind me had me spinning on my heel, coming face to face with Daniel.

Shit.

He looked at me carefully. What was he even doing there?

"You want to tell me what you just meant?" he pushed his hands into his coat pockets.

I was lost for words, and for the first time in my life I couldn't take action. It was Rachel who pulled Daniel into the room and shut the door. How stupid was it to talk about what happened just because Jeff and Amy were safe in a goddamned pantry on the other side of the house?

"Amy let me in," Daniel prompted. He certainly wasn't

reaching for his phone to call the cops, or acting disgusted, or angry.

I still couldn't speak. Rachel stepped forward, glancing at her sleeping sons and pressing her shoulders back. This was a fierce momma in action.

"My husband hurt me and Laurie. One of many. I have no idea who the boy's fathers are, and I don't have to explain why. He tried to stop me leaving when Micah came to rescue me and I shot and killed him."

"No, she didn't," I said, urgently. "It was me. The blame is mine."

Rachel held up a hand. "Stop, Micah. I didn't do anything wrong. I was protecting my babies from a man who nearly killed me."

"You shot him in self-defense," Daniel summarized.

"Yes."

She was daring Daniel to say something, to call the cops, anything, so it was done, and she could deal with it. This is what I should be doing, but I'd seen his expression, he'd looked at me and there was fear in his eyes. I was losing him.

Had I ever had him in the first place?

His expression was unreadable. "You should have told me," he said.

I wanted to argue there was nothing I needed to tell him, that I was protecting my sister, but I'd told him I'd never stopped loving him, and I'd told him we had tomorrows.

He stepped toward me, and hugged me, I wasn't expecting that, and I didn't hug him back when he released me to hug Rachel. They stood together a long time, and he told her he would keep her secret for her sons.

And that was all anyone could ask.

I followed him when he left, all the way to the car, and he never said a word. It could've gone two ways. He could've railed and shouted at me and that was us finished. Or he could've coldly, silently, walked away and that was us finished.

Either way we were done.

At the last minute, by his car he turned to face me and I almost walked into him.

"I did what I had to do for my family," I said, and closed my eyes, waiting for him to hit me, or shout at me, or anything to release the crazy tension between us.

Instead he kissed me, deeply, as if this was the last kiss ever. I clung to him as hard as he did to me, and I didn't want to let him go. *Please don't go.*

We parted and he smiled at me. "I love you," he said.

"Wait? What?"

He smiled then. "You're supposed to say you love me back."

How could he be smiling and joking right now? "This is serious."

He cradled my face and I fought the instinct to yank myself away and let him talk. I owed him that.

"I love you, and what you did for Rachel, and the secret you kept, despite everything. You've kept her safe, and you tried to take the blame even in there, even after she told me what she'd done. I don't blame her for what she did, I can't imagine the fear and pain she must have felt."

"But you're leaving."

"I'm on call, I need to be in town now. I'll come back

tonight, or you and Rachel could come to me, bring the kids. We can talk."

He held me then, and we kissed again, until our lips were hot, but our fingers icy cold. Only then did we separate, and then he left.

All I could think was what he'd said about fear and pain, and Rachel announcing it was her that shot Darren. What happened if others knew? What would happen to Rachel? The kids?

And with absolute certainty I knew what I needed to do.

24

MICAH

I STOOD OUTSIDE THE SHERIFF'S OFFICE FOR SOME TIME, long enough that my hands hurt from the cold.

The place was exactly how I remembered it, a low one-story building tucked behind the diner, with white shutters on the windows. Ivy covered in snow softened the edges and corners. There were empty planters each side of the door, and a noticeboard behind glass full of flyers. There was one for yoga in Collier Springs, one for a mother and toddlers group in the church, another warning readers to lock their bikes. I read all of them twice, and had almost worked up the courage to walk in when the door opened and Neil appeared.

"I wondered when you'd get here." He asked. "Are you coming in?"

He was expecting me? This was the point where I either stayed, or turned and left.

"Yeah," I didn't think anymore, just walked in.

"Micah!"

I stiffened at Daniel calling my name from behind me.

The last person I wanted there was him. He could see through my lies in an instant. He wasn't leaving me any choice though, standing next to me and taking my free hand.

"What are you doing here?" I asked him.

"Chloe said she saw you standing here," Daniel said, "let's go."

"I have something I need to do," I tried to shake off his hold but he really wasn't letting go.

"I think you're going to do something stupid."

"No, I'm doing what is right for Laurie and Oliver."

"We should talk about this," Daniel insisted.

"No." I couldn't be more adamant or focused at that moment and even though Daniel was troubled and wary, he wasn't leaving my side.

"Guys, get your asses in here—it's freezing."

I tried one more time to shake Daniel free and he let go, but only to go through the door and then turn to wait for me. This could've been the last time I'd see him before he watched me throw what we had away. I walked in and Neil shut the door on all of us.

"What's wrong?" He looked from me to Daniel.

"I want to make a report," I said, without introduction.

Neil was confused. "You *and* Daniel?"

Daniel ignored Neil and stood between us. "Don't be stupid."

"I'm her big brother, Daniel."

Neil pushed a hand between us, "What the hell?

"I want Daniel to leave," I said to him.

"Give us the room," Neil said to Daniel and indicated I should go into his office.

"Shit, Micah, no. Neil—"

"Does Micah need a doctor present in the room?" Neil asked and waited.

"For his mental issues, yes," Daniel snapped.

"Please leave the room," Neil asked, politely, but forcefully.

Daniel stood. I could feel his eyes on me. "Please, Micah, don't do anything stupid."

I waited until he'd gone and shut the door before I began to speak.

"I shot a man," I said. As simple as that I began to make a case where Rachel wasn't involved at all. I forged ahead. "You'll find it in your database, a shooting on private land ten miles from Cody, at the Brothers of Chiron compound. I went there to help Rachel and Laurie, and in self-defense I shot and killed a man. A private detective has been to the Lennox Ranch asking questions and before he gets any deeper than just asking, I want this incident finished with my arrest."

That was enough right? He'd pull up the outstanding case, and he would arrest me, and I could do my time, and Rachel and the kids would be safe. Daniel wouldn't understand, but I know if it was Michelle he'd be doing the same thing.

He pulled a notebook toward him and a pen. There was nothing in his posture to indicate he was reaching for a gun, or cuffs, or backup. He looked as calm as if I'd told him my name was Micah.

"Start at the beginning."

"I just told you—"

"The beginning."

"Rachel called me, asked me to collect her from the place she was living, a compound called the Brothers of

Chiron. C. H. I. R. O. N." Neil scribbled words on the paper, but I was too busy watching his expression to see what he was writing. I needed to see that moment when he put all the pieces together.

I continued with as many facts as I could recall. "I found the place quickly, getting to the fence, and seeing the gate. I knew it was the right place, from her directions, but there was nothing there, no signs apart from one warning people they would be prosecuted if they went in. Part forest, part open land, and all along the front there were old rusting cars, like a barrier I guess."

"How did you get in?" Neil asked.

"Bolt cutters in the truck, so yeah, I ignored the sign and trespassed."

Neil nodded as if that made complete sense and I think I'd said enough about what I found when I got there.

"About a hundred feet in or so, there was another gate, as if it had once been the entrance, but whoever lived there wanted that extra ring of protection. That was where I saw the sign for the Brothers of Chiron, some fancy logo with circles. I was ready for anything, and I recall that the area outside the fence was covered in deep snow, no footprints, and no one seemed to have made an effort to clear it. Actually, apart from the new deadlock on the gate it was as though there was no one living there at all. I had the feeling I was being watched, but I did a quick three-sixty and couldn't see anything around me."

"It was evening?"

"Eight, nearly nine."

"What kind of visibility did you have?"

"Enough. I'm used to being out in Wyoming dark," I defended, "And I listened."

"So, you went straight in? No hesitation?"

"I thought about what the hell I was going into. When Rachel called she was desperate, hysterical, her world was imploding, and I didn't know what I was going to find. She kept saying over and over that her husband wouldn't let her go, that none of them would let her go. Then that her husband talked about suicide, and she was scared he would take her and her son with him."

"Why didn't she call the cops?"

"Her husband was in control of her. He said he owned her," I said. That didn't sound dramatic enough to explain the kind of man Callum Prince was. "He was abusive to her and Laurie, and he hid behind religion, to make sure she knew her place. She was a woman alone, desperate and scared for her life and for the lives of her babies, so she reached out to me."

He nodded.

"The door was unlocked, and swung open easily. The floor was wet as if snow had melted inside when it was open, and the place was freezing. I stepped in and saw her the same moment I saw the gun she had pointing at me. She screamed that she was going to kill me, but she didn't see me, she saw someone trying to stop her from leaving, and I just stood there like stone. I noticed Laurie first, hiding behind her legs, not crying, just staring with this horror on his face. Then I saw she was pregnant, it was like a double whammy."

"But she had a gun."

"It was her husband's gun."

"And she finally realized that it was you?"

"I just kept saying, over and over, 'Rachel, it's me', in the same tone I'd use on a frightened horse." I realized I was moving my hands slowly and I looked down at them. God, I was so lost in the moment that I could imagine being there. "She finally lowered the gun, and I took it from her, shoved it into my jacket, and then she fell. I caught her and Laurie behind her and she was crying. Telling me he was coming, that she needed to go, that I had to take Laurie."

"And this was her husband, the one coming."

"Yeah, I assumed that at the time."

Neil made another note on his paper, and this time I watched him write. There wasn't much there, only the key points. I supposed that when I was arrested the interview would be more intense.

"She didn't have any bags, nothing, just Laurie, so I moved to the front door, with Laurie in my arms, supporting Rachel and…" I closed my eyes, trying to remember exactly what had happened and in the order it had happened. "There was this guy in the open door, a gun in his hand and he was wild eyed, frantic, as if he was high. He asked me what was happening, but he didn't really want an answer. There was this hate in his eyes. I remember I moved Laurie to my other hip so the pocket with the gun was accessible." I glanced at Neil. "I'd never used a weapon like that before, but I would if I needed to."

"Okay," Neil said, keeping things simple. I could see the hesitation in him though, and I wondered if *this* was the moment I lost his calm patience and he became the guy who arrested me.

"I identified myself clearly, and this man said Rachel was his wife, and Laurie was *his* son, his property. Over and over. None of it made rational sense at all. I tried to be all alpha male you know, pushed Rachel behind me, turned so I was protecting Laurie, and I fronted like a fucking champion." A scornful snort escaped me. "I wasn't there to be a hero, I just needed to get Rachel out. I pulled the gun and he laughed at me, pointing out he was ready to die anyway. Laurie began to cry and I knew with absolute certainty that I could hurt this man for what he had done to my family."

"So, you shot him?"

"No."

Neil looked relieved, he wouldn't be when he heard the full story I'd created. Everything up until now had been the truth, but from now on it was fabricated.

"He wanted Laurie to go to him, but Laurie was screaming in my ear, and I handed him to Rachel and told her to take him to my car. She was terrified, shouted that others would kill her, and Callum was waving the gun. I said we were leaving, and he'd have to shoot me to stop me. He laughed again, I swear he was on drugs, he was manic with confidence and arrogance and he told me point blank that we'd be stopped before we even got to the Hacklett Bridge."

"Which is where?"

"About eight miles from the compound, maybe more, the edge of town, or so I found out later. I knew for certain one thing at that point. He was going to shoot us all. I knew it as I knew blue skies could bring snow at the drop of a hat. I had the absolute certainty that Rachel's husband was an abusive fucker who hid behind his beliefs to hit his wife and kid and that I was in the firing line."

"But at that point he let you go?"

"I stepped up and over the entry and he crowded me, and fuck, the insanity in his eyes. I've never seen anything like it. We both heard the car door shutting, she'd made it there with Laurie. His weapon wavered as he stared over my shoulder and I hit him square on the nose and he ended up on the floor. I hit him again; he was down, groggy, and I'd dropped the gun. I sprinted to the car, picked the gun, but he lurched for me, and the gun went off. I shot him."

"Where?" This time it was Neil's turn to talk, he'd been so quiet so far.

"The bullet caught him in the neck."

Neil tapped his pen on the pad and judged me with a measured gaze. "Did you stop to check if you could help in any way?"

"Of course, I checked his pulse, he was gone. Laurie was hysterical, and Rachel was sobbing, and I didn't know what to do." I looked at Neil again and he gave me a nod. "There were others there, watching from the dark, a couple of them armed, so I sprinted for the fucking car, vaulted the fence and we left. Drove here."

Neil tapped his pen on the pad, evidently working his way up to whatever he was going to say in summary of this whole situation.

"I have something to show you." He reached into his desk, opened a file in front of him. "The PI came to see me first, wanted to extend all courtesies to local law enforcement in the case, but encouraged me to consider his visit as off-the-record. He gave me enough details that Rachel Lennox was a person of interest and what did I know about her or anyone that had arrived in town with her. He was here to find a missing man, not here to look for you or Rachel."

I knew that, but that didn't matter though. Right? There

still needed to be a guilty party, there was someone who needed to pay.

Neil continued, "I called in a few favors, but even then, things on this case are tied up at a much higher level than I can see. The case is closed, Micah. It was deemed a murder-suicide when more bodies were found in the burned ruins of the house. Most were charred beyond recognition, all except one man who appears to have committed suicide and was found outside. They assume he is the one who killed each member of the cult and then set the fire."

I felt sick. How close had Rachel been to dying? Would they have killed her even though she was pregnant? "How many more died?"

"Two men, four women, two kids, and a baby, forensics indicate poisoning, one man, *your man,* found with a bullet in his throat. There was evidence this was an end of the world religion."

"I don't understand, why isn't this in the news? I checked every day online, every hour."

"Money can smooth a lot of things over. The man who is missing is the son of a US senator, his brother was in the cult. It's not been made public, and I guess this is because of specific political sensitivity." Neil shook his head and sat back in the chair. "They want everything brushed under the carpet, and I'm not filing anything you told me, Micah. You shot a man in self-defense, saving your abused pregnant sister and nephew from a cult that planned to destroy itself for some religious reasons. This case is closed."

"No, you don't understand. I want it on record that it was me, so it doesn't come back to hurt Rachel. Ever."

Neil closed his eyes briefly. "What happened back there is none of my business unless you make it official, if you shot in self-defense, or if Rachel was the one who shot him."

"It was me," I denied, quickly.

"You think I would judge her for what she did? I've seen photos of what was left, Micah, the images will give me nightmares. Don't, for God's sake, make this real. If you do that you expose yourself and your *family* to questions. In that vein, keeping this talk friendly and between us, what do you *want* me to do?"

"It can't be this easy," I said, and paced the office, unable to sit still. "I need to know that Rachel will never be asked questions about the death of her husband." I stopped suddenly and faced Neil head-on. My stomach was in knots, and the pressure building inside me needed to explode. "Can you tell me that?"

Neil shook his head. "I can tell you that the search for the senator's son makes it something out of our control. But there is no case to answer externally for any of the deaths. It's closed, Micah. Leave it." He reached out and shook my hand. "For Rachel, leave it now."

When I left the sheriff's office I found Daniel sitting right outside. He didn't say anything but he stood immediately. We walked out into the cold, and right there in the isolation of a frozen street I told him everything the sheriff had told me.

He listened to every word, and didn't move. When I'd finished I waited for him to comment and he stared at me thoughtfully.

"It's an honorable thing to protect your sister," he murmured.

I immediately went on the defense, “You’re not listening.”

He got up and hugged me as if he was never letting me go.

“No, Micah, I’m really listening for the first time in my life.”

EPILOGUE

MICAH

"You done here?" I asked the young boy with the shovel. He had bright ginger hair, a face full of freckles and his name was Archie. I kid you not. Not that any of this would stop him in life. He was seven but as confident as any sixteen-year-old, all piss and vinegar and ornery as get out when I wouldn't let him do what he wanted.

"I sure am, Mister Lennox," he said and tipped the last shovel full of shit into the barrow. For a small weedy kid, he was strong, and I didn't interfere when he took the handles and carefully made his way out of the barn and over to the heap that would be spread on the far field by tomorrow. He tipped the barrow up and I had to stop myself helping him when he nearly overbalanced and fell on the pile himself.

"Where's your momma?" I asked, aware that yet again Archie was on his own in the barn, with no sight of LouAnne anywhere.

"She has a headache," Archie added a theatrical eye roll to his words. We both knew well enough that the headache was likely due to an overindulgence of wine the night before. She would drive him there, and park at the bottom of the drive and sleep. I didn't know what to do about the fact she likely had alcohol in her system when she was driving, but I had a quiet word with Neil, who said he'd keep an eye out.

Didn't seem to faze Archie though, who went about life as the man of his small family. He cared for his little sister as much as he did his mom and he did it all with a grin and with absolute determination. I loved the little tyke and admired his tenacity, seeing in him a lot of what I'd once had in myself. He was in the second phase of the kids we'd had daily in the summer break. The scheme that Rachel had set up, and she was in charge of admin, and making the lunches.

"Get yourself up to the house for lunch," I said, and waited as he looked back at the horses. There was a pang of longing on his face; he wanted to be with the horses all the time. They were his safe place. I could imagine his thought process as if it were one of my own, horses or food… horses… food. He was as easy to win over as Laurie was with cake.

Finally, it seemed his belly won over and with a last grin he ran to the house. Not jogged, or walked fast. Ran at speed, nearly falling on his ass on the steps. I followed him at a slower pace, and stopped at the bottom of the steps to the large house. We were only ten people there at that time of day. Me, Archie and his sleeping mom, and Rachel and the kids, plus a couple of other hands who were permanent. Sometimes Amy came up from town to help. Retiring didn't seem to suit her, and with the amount of time Jeff spent with the horses, it seemed it didn't suit him either.

The table would be full of food, the laughter genuine from others, and throughout it all I would soak in as much as I could, holding the laughter and affection and keeping it for myself. The Lennox Ranch was tidier, more like the place I'd loved as a child. It was stunning, high in the mountains, the air fresh and clean, which made marketing it easy. Something else that Rachel took care of. She lived in the main house, the old bedroom converted, and added to, until she and the boys had their own space and a huge kitchen all set around the old range that she refused to get rid of.

I couldn't bring myself to think about living in the place, even though it was a different house now. Instead of being filled with sadness, it was a family home. Laurie appeared at the top of the steps, indignant that I wasn't inside yet. He was six now, nearly seven and his Lennox genes were never more obvious than when he was in his summer outfit of jeans and T. With his short blond hair and his pale eyes, he really was a mini-me.

Oliver was into everything, kept Rachel on her toes, and loved his Uncle Scott, who spent a *lot* of time at the house. Scott said he was *in the area*, his usual excuse, but he *was* overseeing the expansion of the log cabins that were sold as soon as people saw the plans.

"Uncle Micah, it will get cold," Laurie insisted. I scooped him up in my arms, held him tight, and he wriggled. Soon he'd be too big for me to hold him like that, he was strong and fit, and worked with the horses like a pro. He was still having counseling the same as Rachel, but his eyes were less haunted. Rachel wasn't doing as well, she had dreams where she hadn't escaped. She said it helped when Scott stayed over. Who was I to argue with that?

At moments like that, if I shut my eyes and inhaled the scent of summer and horses I could've been back on the K, back with Henry Junior, who'd accepted my resignation with sadness. He'd come out and visited, even helped me with building the new barns in our first year, and he was there at Christmas, which had been good. I let the sense memory slip, as Rachel called Laurie, and we focused back on going in for lunch.

When the work day was done, the chores completed, and dinner finished, I was restless and walked down to the Whisper Creek bridge. There had been some work done, moving the road, and there was rubble at the side that I had to clamber over to get to the bridge. I sat on the side of it, dangling my feet over the side and staring down at the water. I ran my thumb over Isaac's name and tried to understand how I was feeling. I had to live in the moment, but I had to respect the past, sound advice from Daniel. I scanned the hill, the road that curved down, which no one would ever be able to use again now it was blocked, and I remembered that night.

The moment I had lost control.

Back to the moment Chris and Isaac were encouraging me to drive faster.

Back again to the moment I'd taken the keys.

And then, back to the second I told Daniel I loved him.

Some of it hurt, some of it made me smile, some if it I couldn't think about yet. I heard a car, recognized the sound of the engine, and I shuffled over a little on the bridge.

This was where I waited for Daniel after work, since the summer afternoons had warmed my bones, and the ice inside had melted. He took a seat next to me and dangled his own legs. We kissed hello and held hands.

"The plumber called," he said.

I chuckled, "I'm so glad you took that one."

"He said, and I quote, 'how can two grown men break a solid shower door for the third time in a month?'"

I looked at our house, the first of Scott's new builds, the closest to the bridge, with a big yard and room enough for both of us. We'd only moved in a month ago, still finding our feet as a couple, but I was happy, and there was chance for more happiness on a daily basis.

"What did you say back to him?"

He bumped shoulders with me, the man I'd loved since I was too young to know any different. "Told him it must be a faulty door."

I side-eyed him. "How the hell did you keep a straight face?"

"It was hard."

We sat in silence for a while, both lost in our thoughts. Every night, or morning if Daniel was called out for any reason, we gave ourselves some time, holding hands, and just *being*. It had worked so far.

"I was thinking today," Daniel murmured, knocking my foot with his to get my attention.

"Dangerous," I smirked.

"Will you marry me?"

The words didn't register at first, and when they did, I didn't have to think for one minute.

"Yes."

He turned to me, and cradled my face, just as he

always did and he smiled at me. “Thank you,” he said, and kissed me.

I lost myself in the kiss, and in the late summer breeze I remembered Isaac, and Chris, and Rachel, and everything made sense.

I was exactly where I should be, and I was happy I’d come back, whatever the reason for returning.

Coming back to the land, to family, and to the man I loved.

THE END

IF YOU LIKED WINTER COWBOY…

Book 2 in the Whisper Ridge series will be available, Summer 2018, meanwhile…

Montana

… you will like my Montana series, with cowboys, a ranch, family, and love.

- Crooked Tree Ranch, Book 1
- The Rancher's Son, Book 2
- A Cowboy's Home, Book 3
- Snow in Montana, Book 4

Crooked Tree Ranch, Montana, Book 1

When a cowboy meets the guy from the city, he can't know how much things will change.

On the spur of the moment, with his life collapsing around him, Jay Sullivan answers an ad for a business manager with an expertise in marketing, on a dude ranch in Montana.

With his sister, Ashley, niece, Kirsten and nephew, Josh, in tow, he moves lock stock and barrel from New York to Montana to start a new life on Crooked Tree Ranch.

Foreman and part owner of the ranch, ex rodeo star Nathaniel 'Nate' Todd has been running the dude ranch, for five years ever since his mentor Marcus Allen became ill.

His brothers convince him that he needs to get an expert in to help the business grow. He knows things have to change and but when the new guy turns up, with a troubled family in tow - he just isn't prepared for how much.

The Texas series

The Heart of Texas

Riley Hayes, the playboy of the Hayes family, is a young

man who seems to have it all: money, a career he loves, and his pick of beautiful women. His father, CEO of HayesOil, passes control of the corporation to his two sons; but a stipulation is attached to Riley's portion. Concerned about Riley's lack of maturity, his father requires that Riley *'marry and stay married for one year to someone he loves'*.

Angered by the requirement, Riley seeks a means of fulfilling his father's stipulation. Blackmailing Jack Campbell into marrying him "for love" suits Riley's purpose. There is no mention in his father's documents that the marriage had to be with a woman and Jack Campbell is the son of Riley Senior's arch rival. Win win.

Riley marries Jack and abruptly his entire world is turned inside out. Riley hadn't counted on the fact that Jack Campbell, quiet and unassuming rancher, is a force of nature in his own right.

This is a story of murder, deceit, the struggle for power, lust and love, the sprawling life of a rancher and the whirlwind existence of a playboy. But under and through it all, as Riley learns over the months, this is a tale about family and everything that that word means.

HAVE YOU READ THE HEROES SERIES?

A series of three books featuring a SEAL, a Marine and a Cop, and the guys that fall for them...

A Reason To Stay - Book 1

featuring Viktor from Sanctuary

When SEAL, Viktor Zavodny, left small town America for the Navy he made sure he never had a reason to return for anything other than visiting family. He wanted to see the world and fight for his country and nothing, or no one, was getting in his way. He fights hard, and plays harder, and a succession of men and women share his bed.

But a phone call from his sister has him using his thirty

day down time to go home instead of enjoying his usual thirty nights of random sex and sleep.

What he finds is a mystery on the Green Mountains and the only man attempting to make sense of seemingly unrelated deaths. His childhood friend and first love... Lieutenant Aiden Coleman, Sheriff.

There were reasons Viktor left his home. Not least Aiden Coleman with his small town innocence and his dreams of forever. Now Adam and Viktor need to work together to save lives and prove there is a hero in all of us.

When it's done, if they make it out alive, can Aiden persuade Viktor that he has a reason to stay? Maybe forever?

Also in this completed series

- Last Marine Standing - Book 2
- Deacons Law - Book 3

MEET RJ SCOTT

RJ's goal is to write stories with a heart of romance, a troubled road to reach happiness, and most importantly, that hint of a happily ever after.

RJ Scott is the bestselling author of over one hundred romance books and is known for writing books that always end with a happy ever after.

She lives just outside London and spends every waking minute she isn't with family either reading or writing.

The last time she had a week's break from writing she didn't like it one little bit.

She has yet to meet a bottle of wine she couldn't defeat.

www.rjscott.co.uk
rj@rjscott.co.uk

facebook.com/author.rjscott
twitter.com/Rjscott_author
instagram.com/rjscott_author

Made in the USA
Middletown, DE
30 September 2018